❊ ❊ ❊

Life looked bleak to pretty Norah Oliver with her widowed mother seriously ill, her brother and herself out of jobs—only her sister's meager salary keeping the little family from starvation.

If only David would marry her, how grand things would be—but David had been strangely indifferent of late.

And then Norah hit upon the fantastic idea of advertising herself as a "wife for sale." . . .

Life changed quickly to an exciting whirl when Barry Dunsmuir answered her ad.

Norah's daring adventure makes a fascinating story of love and its strange ways with a girl and the two men who worshiped her.

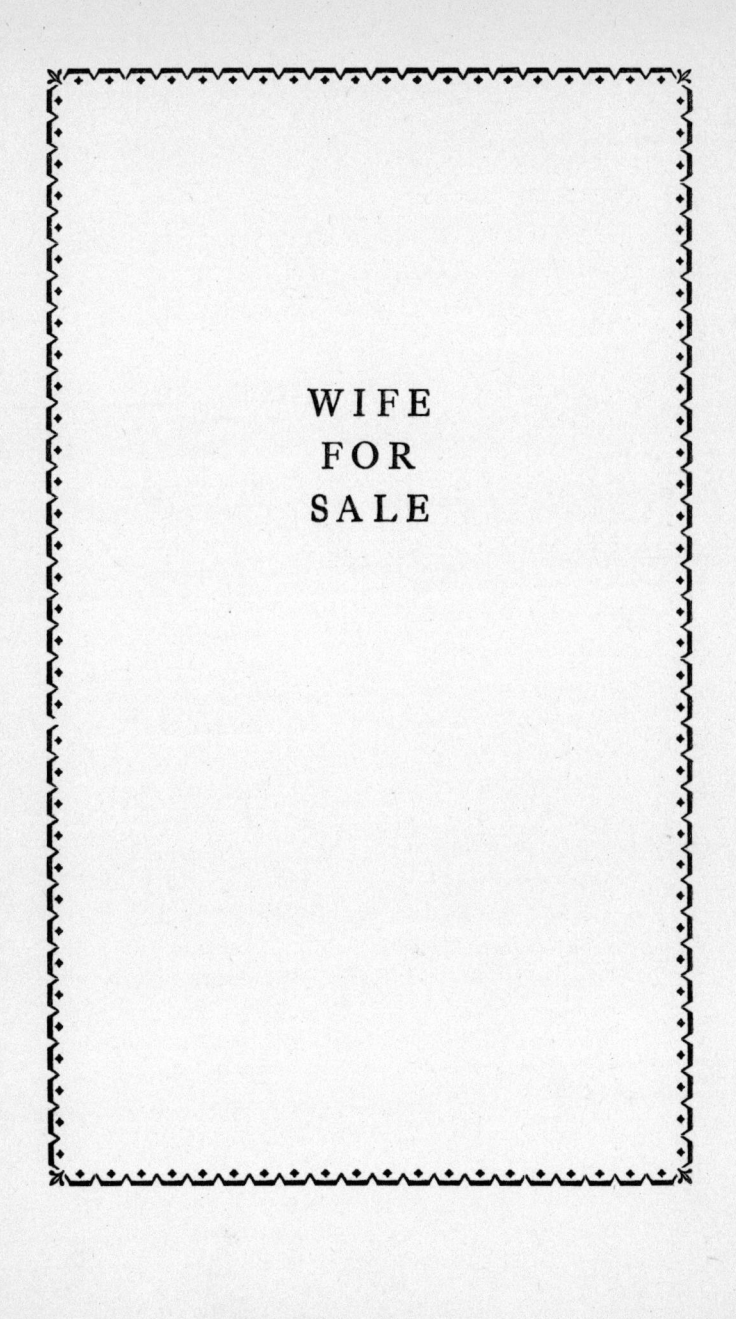

WIFE
FOR
SALE

BOOKS BY
KATHLEEN NORRIS

Wife for Sale
My California
Walls of Gold
Treehaven
My San Francisco
Younger Sister
Second Hand Wife
Belle-Mère
The Love of Julie Borel
Hands Full of Living
Beauty in Letters
The Lucky Lawrences
Margaret Yorke
Passion Flower
Red Silence
Storm House
The Foolish Virgin
What Price Peace?
Beauty and the Beast
The Fun of Being a Mother
My Best Girl
Barberry Bush
The Sea Gull
Hildegarde

The Black Flemings
Little Ships
Mother and Son
Home
Noon
Rose of the World
The Callahans and the Murphys
Butterfly
Certain People of Importance
Lucretia Lombard
The Beloved Woman
Harriet and the Piper
Sisters
Josselyn's Wife
Undertow
Martie, The Unconquered
The Heart of Rachel
The Story of Julia Page
The Treasure
Saturday's Child
Poor, Dear Margaret Kirby
The Rich Mrs. Burgoyne
Mother

KATHLEEN NORRIS

WIFE FOR SALE

1933
Doubleday, Doran & Company, Inc.
Garden City, New York

PRINTED AT THE *Country Life Press*, GARDEN CITY, N. Y., U. S. A.

COPYRIGHT, 1932, 1933
BY KATHLEEN NORRIS
ALL RIGHTS RESERVED

FIRST EDITION

For MARY WALDRON FAIRFOWL
Sicut erat in principio, et nunc, et semper.

WIFE
FOR
SALE

Chapter I

NORAH OLIVER closed the door of her mother's bedroom noiselessly behind her and looked vaguely, disconsolately, about the little apartment-house kitchen. She crossed to the table, sat down at it, with her elbows on the oilcloth and her chin cupped in her hands, and for a long while stared into space.

The prospect within her immediate line of vision was anything but inspiring, but Norah saw none of it. She was completely unaware of the actual scene about her: her mind was many miles away.

It was four o'clock on a winter afternoon; in the kitchen dusk had already descended. The kitchen window commanded an irregular airshaft, whose shape was determined by rising tenement walls and jutting angles or fire escapes and neighboring kitchen windows. Garbage tins, old brooms and dangling lines of washed clothes variously decorated the prospect, and beyond them and above them hung a heavy roof of dark sky.

By hanging out of the window anyone in the Oliver flat could see the flooring of the shaft carpeted deep in old rags, rubbish, papers, tins, five flights below. Noises were usually ascending from this area: voices, crying, victrolas, the hissing of running water, the sizzle of frying food. Odors often mounted too; the Olivers knew when the Hungarians on the second floor were frying onions in oil and when the Reilleys were having boiled cabbage.

Neither noises nor odors disturbed Norah today. She was sunk in despairing thought. Life had never been particularly easy for her, but somehow she had always taken it serenely enough until just lately, until this last year or two. Now it seemed to be getting harder and darker and more puzzling day by day. Norah felt tired and bewildered. She spoke aloud in the silent kitchen, "I don't know what to do!"

A hurt and angry expression gradually took possession of her face; her eyes filled slowly with tears. She made no effort to wipe the tears away, but let them run down her cheeks, and continued to sit at the table, with her elbows on the oilcloth and her chin in her hands.

"I feel—beaten!" she finally whispered. And then, bestirring herself and getting to her feet, she added sensibly, "This doesn't do any good! I might as well get to work!"

An invalid's tray, with tea gray and cooling in a cup and a remnant of cold buttered toast upon it, was standing upon the table. There were unwashed dishes in the sink, and packages from the grocery were piled upon the sink board: a box of eggs, three cans of tomatoes, bread, potatoes that had rolled from their bag and left earthy streaks.

All these demanded Norah's too familiar care. She attacked them patiently, if wearily. Dishes and dishes: they never were done. Why weren't there wood-fiber dishes in pretty designs that could be burned after every meal? Her active brain played with the idea as she cleared the tray and arranged it for the next little meal. Mother's doctor had said "light nourishment every three or four hours." She had had tea and toast at two o'clock, at six she might have—she might have the rest of the soup—and crackers and cream cheese——

When her mother was ill Norah loved to take care of her, and washing dishes for an invalid was the least one could do.

But, seriously, why shouldn't dishes be pretty and firm and yet cheap enough to be destroyed daily? Every household would have to have an incinerator then. "And of course," Norah reflected, "it isn't only the dishes: it's putting things away, and washing lettuce, and saving the ends of butter——"

She filled the heavy kettle and put it on the stove, lighting a gas flame under it. There never was much hot water on Mondays, because all the women in the house washed on that day. Something had been spilled on the stove tray: no use to let it stay there and begin to sizzle and smell. Norah carried the tray to the sink and added it to the confusion there.

The potatoes were tumbled with a little rush of earthy dust into a box on the fire escape; Norah reserved three to bake. Keith would eat one, Eve would eat part of one—better make it three, for Keith might be extra hungry. The rest of the dinner would be the stew.

She took it in from the ice box: it looked frozen and grease-flaked; it smelled bleakly of cold onion, cold turnip. If it were made very hot, of course, or if she made a nice fluffy crust with which to cover it—it could bake while the potatoes were baking——

"Why doesn't someone invent a canned pie crust?—pastry is such a pest!" Norah thought idly, resentfully. She reviewed the menu for the evening meal unenthusiastically: "Stew, baked potatoes, bread, tea, doughnuts, and there are prunes, if anyone wants them, and there are oranges."

Disgusting gloomy afternoon; disgusting airshaft, all noises and smells; disgusting apartment house in a slummy street. What a horrible world this world could be! And if Norah Oliver, twenty-four years old, thought so, how much more horrible it must seem to the sick persons in the house and the mothers with lots of children to bring up.

Mrs. Flynn had made this smelly, stiff, cold stew on Saturday, when she had come to clean the house. It had been a pot roast then; both Eve and Keith had approved of it. Yesterday it had been a re-heated pot roast, but Mother hadn't wanted any; Keith had been away, of course, with Anne, Larry Carter had taken off Eve for dinner, and Norah had been satisfied to share the second-day meat with Uncle Rodney, who had turned up as usual at just about dinner time.

Now, awaiting its third appearance, it seemed to Norah positively revolting.

"I wonder what Mother would do with this? She always has things so nice."

And Norah determined that when her mother called her she would ask the question. Presently Mrs. Oliver did call, feebly and thickly, from the adjoining bedroom, and Norah went in.

Darkness was in the sick-room, and the odors of flannel and medicine. The form on the bed stirred.

"Awake, darling?"

"I was only drowsing. What time is it, Norah?"

"About five. Any pain?"

"Just—" Mrs. Oliver laughed feebly—"just

comfortable pain!" she said. "It's nothing after yesterday. I'll be up tomorrow."

"Yes, you will!" the daughter scoffed affectionately. She straightened covers, snapped up a light. "Hungry?" she asked.

"Well, not entirely indifferent to food," the sick woman admitted cheerfully. "And I feel very guilty," she added, "keeping you away from your job in these times with jobs what they are."

Norah made no comment upon this; she was putting a neat stack of magazines on a table shelf. But she managed a reassuring shrug and a smile.

Her mother looked at her sharply as the girl turned again toward the bed.

"Norah. You've been crying?"

Norah sat down on the edge of the bed, and laid her hand over the older woman's frail one.

"Don't you know that you oughtn't to notice things like that, my dear child?"

"What's making you blue?" her mother countered, by way of answer, in a concerned and tender tone.

"Nothing special," Norah answered composedly, after thought.

"Is it David?"

The girl, looking down, raised her eyelashes for a quick look.

"Partly, maybe."

"Where is he now, Norah?"

WIFE FOR SALE

"Where is he, Mother?" Norah was honestly surprised.

"Yes. Is he right here—at home, I mean, over on Park Avenue?"

"Why, I suppose so. I don't know anything to the contrary."

Mrs. Oliver considered this for a moment of silence; her anxious eyes did not leave her daughter's face.

"Funny!" she presently said unhappily.

"Is it?" Norah asked. "Aren't men always doing that—rushing girls—liking them for a while, and then wondering how they can ease it off most quickly and most completely?"

"You didn't quarrel, dear?"

"Ah—if we had!" Norah half laughed, half wailed.

"It was Daddy's death, it was our moving to this dreadful place," the mother said restlessly. "You were in mourning, you were working when most of the girls David knew were just having a good time——"

"I was working when I met Dave."

"Yes, I know. But Daddy was living then; we had a so much nicer place."

Norah sat silent, rubbing her mother's hand with her firm young thumb.

"You don't think David—cares any more, dear?"

The girl spoke steadily in a voice of pain.

"I'm afraid I know he doesn't, Mother. I'm not going to—to die of it. I like him—tremendously, better than any man I've ever seen. But I've done all I can to—let him know. I've telephoned—I've telephoned his house—and gotten his mother, very polite and clear and cool! I've written him little notes—on one excuse or another, and I sent him a book we had talked about."

A silence. Then Norah added:

"I can't do any more than that, can I?"

Her mother was silent, her delicate, sensitive face full of trouble.

"If we could have him here and have a nice little dinner in the dining room——" she began, and hesitated.

"The last time he came," Norah recalled, "Keith was to be here and balance the table, and Keith had to work and didn't come home. Old Mrs. Francis came, and we had to keep her for dinner. It was the hottest May night since the weather bureau began keeping statistics. And the Reilleys' victrola and the Andulian baby had their semifinals down the airshaft!

"No," Norah ended, as her mother, distressed, did not speak. "I'll get over it, and a lot of other things, and everything will come out all right. If a man doesn't want to stand by me in hard times, he isn't my man after all. David's young, and he's popular—everyone is making a fuss about him—it's natural enough! I've just got to put him out of my mind, that's all!"

"It's all so hard for you," the mother mourned. "If you had pretty gowns and could accept nice invitations——

"But as it is," she added, "I don't see how we dare move. Keith was talking to me so seriously yesterday: he says that Baker & Bayne may have to lay off more men—he doesn't say for *long,* of course, but I could see it worried him."

"Did Keith say that?" Norah asked in an odd voice. But she waited for no answer. With a cheerful reference to soup and crackers she abruptly rose, and her mother could presently hear her humming cheerfully as she busied herself in the kitchen.

After a while she heard the outer door slam, and Keith's voice, sonorous, magnificent.

"Come, my good girl, this sort of shilly-shallying will get you nowhere! What's that intended to be?"

Norah's answer came tremblingly, obsequiously:

"It's a meat pie, your worship. I thought your worship might relish some of our country beef."

"Look to it then, wench!" Keith said sternly. "And mind you keep a civil tongue in your head!" And crossing to the bedroom doorway he went on, "Hello, how's the good old slacker tonight?"

"Keith, that's exactly what I am!" the mother protested, with a deprecatory laugh.

"Better, huh?" he asked, kissing her.

"Why, I'm perfectly well! And Norah came home at noon to take care of me—made me so ashamed——"

Norah, in the kitchen, could hear the affectionate murmur rise and fall; then Keith went on to the bathroom and was to be heard ejaculating, "Damn Monday!" after a brief trial of the hot-water faucet.

Other familiar sounds echoed through the house. Men were coming home tired; children were skimming off on last errands to the grocery. Victrolas droned, and radios were started up everywhere. The Cahill children in the kitchen next door went into spasms of whooping, and downstairs somewhere there were angry words, a crash of pottery and a wild gush of sizzling—burning—steaming.

"Now look what you done, Joe!" a woman screamed. Mrs. Oliver heard it, and she looked into Norah's eyes, as Norah put a tempting little tray before her, and gently shook her head.

"We'll be glad to get out of *here*," she said.

Eve came in, tired and jaded and drooping. She was very pale tonight, and said that the subway had given her a sort of headache, she thought. Like the others, she paid her mother a brief visit. Dinner was served immediately.

"We eat in the kitchen?" Eve asked wearily, indifferently.

"Keith's going out. He's dressing."

Norah called, "Keith, hurry up!" as she put the meat pie on the table. Eve poured herself a cup of strong tea.

"You're dead tonight, aren't you?" Norah asked sympathetically. The younger girl's eyes filled; she raised her head proudly.

"Oh, I don't know," she answered airily.

"I was wondering," Norah said, as she went to and fro, "why we don't turn the sitting room into Keith's room and have the dining room and sitting room in one. I saw a darling place in *Country Homes* today, and they had their meals at the end of the drawing room, with a fireplace and windows and everything!"

"And you think our dining room might be made like that!" Eve tried to say scornfully. But she was too tired to achieve it; her voice faltered into silence, and she devoted herself to her tea, looking as if she wanted to cry. Eve was fair and pretty and fastidious at nineteen; Norah's heart ached fiercely when she saw Eve's blue eyes redden, and heard Eve's voice thicken, and realized—as she had had to realize so often of late!—that Eve was unhappy.

No, Norah knew their wretched dark box of a dining room could not ever look like that California bungalow in the book, and she felt discouraged again. Luckily, as she sat down to dinner, Keith came out, and the conversation became general.

"You came home early?"

"About one."

"Want to go to a picture with me and Anne?"

Norah's face brightened: she had always adored her brother, and to have him so especially nice to her was heartening.

"Hadn't you better ask Anne?"

"No," Keith said, grinning, "we'll take a chance on Anne."

"I'm going to stay home, anyway," Eve volunteered, and she and Norah presently had almost a fight about the dishes, Eve saying, "Oh, do, for heaven's sake, go on, Norah: there's nothing to this," and Norah persisting, "No, I won't leave you all this to clear up!"

It was a little after eight when she and Keith were down in the street walking toward Anne's house. Anne taught school; she was an idolized only daughter, who lived with her parents and grandparents in a much nicer neighborhood than the Olivers'.

They went past the shabby apartment-house doorways and the lighted little cheap shops, along the dark wintry sidewalks where gum was frozen in dull overlapping rings and the dirty remains of snow lurked sootily in cornices and cracks. When they got to the public library

WIFE FOR SALE

Keith said, "Come in here a minute, Norah. I want to talk to you without Mother hearing us."

Norah entered with him the big warm room that was so pleasantly sheltered after the unfriendly streets, and they sat down in a secluded corner. Keith's manner by this time was causing his sister vague uneasiness, and she looked at him expectantly, and even with a little apprehension.

"What's the matter, Keith?"

"Nothing's the matter," the boy said, with a reassuring laugh. Nothing ever really frightened Keith; Norah had complete faith in him. "But here's the thing," he said: "I've lost my job. This is the—what is it, the sixth? I go out on the first of December."

Norah's gray eyes widened; she turned a little pale.

"Keith! You don't!"

"Old Bayne told me last week, but I wouldn't tell Mother. I've only been there two years. It's all right—shucks, I'll get something else," Keith said easily.

"But, listen," the girl said. "I didn't tell Mother either, or anyone. But I'm fired, too."

Their eyes were riveted together for a long time. Then they both laughed briefly.

"For help's sake!" the boy observed.

"So, Keith," the girl said anxiously, "what shall we *do?*"

"Fired, hey?" Keith mused. "Who said so?"

"Mr. Locox."

"What'd he say?"

"Oh, the usual bunk. They all liked me, and I had been entirely satisfactory. I notice they didn't fire Yvonne!"

"She's the girl friend?"

"Well," Norah modified it, a little ashamed, "we think so."

"Ha!" Keith exclaimed. "The plot thickens. When do you get out?"

"Today. With one week's pay—twenty-two dollars. Oh, I don't blame them," Norah said, "I know how things have been going. But when I think of Mother——"

"Oh, Mother won't care! She's a good old trooper," Keith said, unalarmed.

"Yes, but you too now, Keith. Neither one of us working! What'll we live on?"

"We won't starve," he said, thinking.

"I don't know why not," Norah said in her soul. Aloud she said nothing, but continued to look at her brother intently and expectantly.

"My forty-five a week and your twenty-two came out sixty-seven," Keith mused. "Eve gets——?"

"Sixteen."

"Help!" he ejaculated faintly.

"And rent sixty," Norah offered.

"Rent sixty. And Mother sick."

"Mother," the girl pronounced, "ought to

have care and rest and nourishing food for weeks. It was *almost* pneumonia."

"Righto," Keith agreed absently. He was deep in thought again.

"Keith," Norah asked impulsively, "what's the matter with us?"

He looked at her, scowling. Keith was often impatient with Norah; she suspected that he thought her visionary and sentimental and everything that he was not. Quailing a little, she repeated her question.

"I mean—something must be the matter!" she went on, a little flatly. "We're decent and we work hard and we just—just can't get along."

Tears came into her eyes.

"Other people get along," she submitted timidly.

Keith's forehead darkened.

"That kind of talk doesn't get us anywhere!" he said disapprovingly.

"I know," Norah agreed quickly, her heart shriveling in the fashion it had when Keith was stern. "But you can't help thinking—or at least I can't—that there's something wrong with us. We're not the sort that—that succeeds, that gets anywhere. Other people have experiences—trips and marriages and adventures; we just stay in our groove. There's nothing I do well—I'm not a nurse or a teacher or a professional woman——"

"Don't cry!" Keith warned her, in an embarrassed undertone, with a glance about.

Norah realized that she had indeed commenced to cry. She wiped her eyes surreptitiously and smiled apologetically at her brother. It was no fun for him either, poor Keith, with all of them on his hands!

And suddenly she realized that he was sympathizing with her; that he was going to be nice.

"It's tough on you, you poor kid!" he said a little gruffly, looking away.

Norah's lip shook, and her eyes filled again.

"If only you could know when it was going to *stop,*" she began shakily. "If only we knew that it would all come out right!"

Keith considered this frowningly.

"Well, doesn't it, usually?" he asked youthfully, after a pause.

"I mean," he added, as Norah merely looked at him inquiringly and expectantly, "don't people usually come out on top when they're straight, and ambitious, and willing to work hard? Don't all the books say so?"

"Oh, the books!" Norah observed, with a shrug.

"Aren't we due for a break?" the boy persisted.

Suddenly into her unreasonable Irish heart Norah felt happiness coming in a flood. It wasn't so bad to be young, and poor, and deep in confidential conference with an adored brother. Courage returned; they would conquer the world yet!

"Well, we are. And we'll be laughing at all this, this time next year!" she predicted boldly. "But the thing is, Keith, *jobs,*" Norah concluded impressively.

"I went to see a fellow about one this afternoon," Keith observed suddenly. Norah's expressive eyes lighted.

"A job?"

"Yep. He asked me if I'd go to Guatemala."

"Guatemala!" Life was roseate to Norah for a dazzling minute. "You couldn't?" she asked, her face falling as she read his expression. "You said no?"

"It was only a hundred a month and expenses. I couldn't take Anne on that, and I couldn't leave her."

"Ah—Anne." Norah was conscious of a little chill of fear. If Keith once assumed the obligation of caring for Anne, then who would look out for Mother and Eve and Norah?

Keith, looking at her, asked suddenly in a somewhat self-conscious voice:

"All off with you and Dave Howard?"

Norah returned his stare steadily; her elbows were on the table again; her round, firm chin in her palms.

"Inasmuch as it ever was on, yes," she answered, outwardly unruffled. But her soul within her was sick.

"Don't see him any more?"

"No."

"So that he's out of it," Keith mused. Norah would have given ten years off the end of her life to be able to say honestly, "He wanted to marry me, Keith, and I couldn't!" or at least, "He feels very badly." She said nothing.

"Well," Keith presently resumed, "what now? There's Mother needing care and freedom from worry; there's Eve, she hates her job, and she only makes sixteen a week; there's you and there's me. Gosh—if we only had an uncle or a bank account——"

"There's Uncle Rod!" Norah reminded him, and giggled youthfully. Keith looked at her again, and saw her prettiness and smallness and courage suddenly; her fine pale skin and gray eyes, her smart little hat, and the even line of her square teeth.

"You're awfully game, Nono," he said. Radiance poured into Norah's face, and her heart swelled with joy. She didn't care how hard times were if only her own people loved her!

"You see, Keith," she said eagerly, and he thought he had never seen Norah so endearing and so pretty, "there are lots of things I could do, if I had a chance. But—to get that chance!"

"What sort of things?"

"Oh," she said largely, "anything! I could open a school, or I could have a roadside inn and serve chicken dinners. Or I could do marionettes, or open a chintz shop—or I could cook lunches for people! Anything—*anything!* I'd go be a nurse, Keith, if it weren't for leaving Mother, or —if we had one single extra inch in the apartment I could take boarders."

Her gray eyes sparkled at him; she was very much in earnest.

"But how to get started!" she lamented. "We have five rooms, we four, and there are boxes under all the beds, and bundles on all the closet shelves. Boarders—well, they'd have to sleep in the kitchen. I couldn't cook for private orders on that little stove—I couldn't take in babies to board and have them fall off the fire escape."

"No, you couldn't—not very long you couldn't."

"So what to *do,* Keith? In the old days women had gardens and chickens and fruit and attics, plenty of space to develop ideas. Even jam: you could make a fortune on home-made jam! But imagine me trying to boil it and bottle it in that kitchen."

They looked at each other. After a moment Keith said uncertainly, "But somehow I don't see us living anywhere but in the city."

"Well, since Father died, we always *have* lived in the city," Norah observed moderately.

"Remember going down to Good Ground or somewhere every summer when we were kids?"

"Ah, don't I!" Her anxious eyes softened. "Doesn't it seem like a dream now?—Dad—and old Nellie cooking for us!"

"It seems like a dream that we ever had enough money."

"Or that anyone ever has enough!" Norah said.

"You see, I kind of hate to spring this on Mother, Norah, about our both being fired, I mean, until we've got some good news."

"I know.

"What would happen, Keith," the girl asked suddenly, after a silence during which they both had been thinking hard, "if you put an advertisement in the paper: 'Will some rich man invest in a poor family who will repay him as soon as possible'?"

"You'd get a lot of fortune-tellers' cards and some millinery ads," Keith predicted, and Norah laughed.

"We don't know one soul who could help us, Keith, do we?"

"Nope."

"As for poor old Uncle Rod, he's on the brink of landing himself on us for life, he as much as said so yesterday."

"Ha!" Keith ejaculated. "Well," he said, "there's no use worrying. We'll scout around for a few days and see what we can scare up, and then we'll break it to Mother."

"Even if we have to take less, Keith, we'll *have* to get jobs."

"Oh, sure. Take anything!"

They went out into the dark street again and turned toward Anne's house. Norah clung to her brother's arm; she had always wished he never would marry, and that they could live together some day, just he and she. She was jealous of Anne, though she never let him see it. Anne seemed to feel that she was doing Keith Oliver a favor to let him admire her. Anne was two years younger than Norah, which made Anne's complacent little airs especially trying.

"We'll get out of this all right, won't we, Keith?" Norah asked for the tenth time, when they had rung Anne's bell.

"Oh, sure we will!"

Chapter II

EARLY on Sunday morning, just as dim winter dawn was fumbling at her window, Norah awoke, and lay thinking, with her body stretched luxuriously under the warm bedding, and her hands locked on the pillow under her head.

She thought of business buildings, of elevators, of politely interested clerks at waiting-room desks. She saw herself, Norah Oliver, in her worn, well brushed dark blue suit and blue hat, advancing to these desks in her turn, asking quietly—not too assuredly, to see Mr. Moore, or Miss Ingalls, or Miss Hudson. Was it about employment? Yes, about employment.

The impassive faces, the civil voices, the sharp pencils with which Miss Ingalls or Miss Hudson or Mr. Moore would write down one more name and address! One more girl "looking for work."

Funny world, this, Norah thought. Once you got a job, how you hated it! But when you had no job, what a glamour spread itself over just being employed, just being out of the lines of waiting and asking!

She had had several jobs and had hated them all. To be shut in an office all day, to breathe office air, scented with radiator pipes, typewriter oil, and pencil dust, to file things, write things, copy things, was dull employment. To slip out to a cafeteria lunch and be back to punch a time clock in exactly thirty minutes was to be only a stupid cog in a stupid machine. That wasn't living; that wasn't worth doing. And yet, how scrupulously it had to be done, all this mumbo-jumbo of modern efficiency, and how hard it was not to show one's boredom at the "pep talks," the "employee conferences" which were all a part of it!

Ah, but there was the twenty-two-dollar check at the end of the week to consider. That was very important. And according to everyone who ever spoke authoritatively on the subject, and according to everything Norah had ever read, even the humblest job might lead to fame and fortune some day.

Well, no job of hers had ever seemed likely to do so, and here she was now, on a dark morning some few weeks before Christmas, lying awake in the bed she shared with Eve, and obliged to consider the position of having no job at all and no prospect of one, and no money, and no friends with money.

More disquieting still, Keith, the family rock of comfort and safety, had no job either. Norah winced when she thought of Keith. Perhaps he was getting tired of the too-heavy load his father's death had imposed upon him. Or perhaps boys took their responsibilities less seriously than girls did.

At all events, during the past trying week, when he and Norah had both tramped their respective discouraging ways into business buildings, up in elevators, past hall clerks' desks, Keith had shown an increasing, rather than lessening, concern over the whole problem. He had spoken more than once of the Guatemala prospect.

"If Anne and I once got down there, there might be lots of ways I could pick up a little extra money!"

And, "Anne says her uncles would be bound to send her checks instead of wedding presents, and they'd help for a while, anyway!"

This from Keith, who had always been so sternly devoted to his own people, filled Norah's heart with despair.

"It's Anne, of course!" Eve explained it lightly, in her bored, sweet young voice. "She's probably kissing all the sense he ever had out of him! Her cousin Lily told me Anne was going to be married soon; right away, she said. 'To my brother,' I told her, and of course Lily looked like a fool. She is a fool, anyway!

"Anne doesn't care what becomes of us," Eve went on, as Norah, whose idol was tottering, preserved a troubled silence. "She'd love to get married and go to Guatemala!"

"Well, for that matter, so would I," Norah interpolated.

"I'd love to go anywhere," Eve adapted it. "And I'd marry darned near anyone!"

Norah laughed, but it was rather a forlorn laugh.

"I wonder if we would?" she said.

"Would what?"

"Marry anyone."

"Well, I wouldn't marry a Jamaican darky with leprosy," Eve observed.

"No—but you know how it is in the old novels, Eve, Trollope and Miss Yonge, and all that old stuff of Mother's! Girls were always marrying for money then."

"There wasn't anything else for them to do in those days."

"Well," and Norah laughed again, "is there now?"

"You must feel awfully flat, marrying for money," the younger sister mused.

"Just the same, I'll bet lots of men would gladly do it!" Norah said, an odd light in her gray eyes.

She had thought about it all that day and all through the next day, and she thought about it on Sunday morning, lying in bed. And on Sunday night, when Keith was out and Eve had gone to a movie with Larry Carter, Norah got out her writing materials and sat down at the kitchen table and entered into the serious business of composition.

"Wanted: by an American girl of 24, gray eyes, light brown hair, a man who———"

Norah paused, captivated by a new idea. Why not make it a letter, to the forum of open letters the newspaper published every day? That wouldn't cost anything and would reach a wider public.

Inspired, she could go straight ahead now; her mother, drowsy under a sleeping pill, heard the old typewriter clicking busily.

"What are you doing, darling?"

"Writing an ad, Mother!"

"Dear Editor of the Forum," wrote Norah, and in sheer excitement she laughed aloud.

"Dear Editor of the Forum: I am an American girl twenty-four years old, healthy, and sufficiently good-looking, with light brown hair and gray eyes. My family has played an honorable part in the history of this country, my grandfather and uncles being respectively a general in the army, a lawyer of some repute, and a doctor. My father was a court reporter whose health failed about three years ago.

"Well, that last isn't quite true," Norah thought, interrupting herself. "Dad was a wholesale chemist, and he's dead. But I can't give myself away!"

She went back to the letter, relishing its lofty phrases, *"sufficiently good-looking . . . played an honorable part in the history of this country . . ."*

"To support my father during a long convalescence," she typed on, *"I would be glad to find a man of similar good lineage and honest intentions, who would give me a certain sum of money —say twenty thousand dollars, which might be invested in my father's favor, or purchase him an annuity. In return I would marry this man, if he liked me, and make him as good a wife as I possibly could. I am a good cook and have had stern training in domestic economy; I love dancing, the theater, and hospitality.*

"As a guarantee of my integrity——

"Maybe that sounds too businesslike," thought Norah, stopping short.

"To show that I am in earnest," she substituted, after a moment's reflection, *"I may say that my religion forbids second marriage and frowns on divorce, so that I would have every reason to regard this marriage as a serious step,*

and to use every possible means in my power to make it a success. I would hope to repay my husband for his generosity by giving him a good home, children, friends, and my lifelong devotion.

"There!" Norah said aloud in satisfaction, jerking the page from the machine.

"Did you call me, Norah?" her mother's voice said drowsily from the bedroom.

"I just said 'there'!" Norah called back.

She read her letter over and was pleased with it. Now to find a perfectly blank envelope and address it in typewriting, which told no tales. And now for signing.

This took more thought. Finally Norah wrote at the bottom of the page the words: *"Wife for Sale."* She put a stamp on the envelope and ran down to the dark street to post it, in the night.

Norah read the "Open Forum" of the newspaper every morning for a week; there was no mention of "Wife for Sale," and it was one more note in a depressing time that she had to conclude that even this desperate offer had made no impression; had merely been swept away in the discarded mass of the big daily's mail.

The weather turned bitterly cold, and winds blew over the dirty streets and tangled newspapers against the columns of the elevated trains. The subways were hot and smelled of pipes and steam, and the little red eye of the electric stove in her mother's room was shining day and night.

Norah went up in elevators into big buildings and talked to civil clerks at hall desks. She was offered ten dollars a week and commissions for selling advertising on a new magazine; she was asked if she thought she could put up good sales talks about a patent medicine that was a palpable fraud. She tried theatrical agencies. She followed up a promising advertisement that began *"Big money for girls, 18 to 30, High School Graduates only,"* and discovered that the High School Graduates must each have one hundred dollars to pay down for learning a new system of teaching languages.

In the late afternoons profound discouragement and fatigue would take possession of her, and she would look at her remaining addresses without enthusiasm. They could wait until tomorrow; it was after three o'clock now, nearly four, indeed, and Mother was alone. Norah would go home, to make tea, to share a hot cup of it with her mother, to huddle in a chair in the warm bedroom, lazy, comfortable, almost in a trance.

Her money was steadily diminishing; Keith's was diminishing too; there seemed to be nothing to do about it. They could only go on searching for jobs; families like the Olivers did not steal and they did not beg.

"And anyway," as Eve put it simply, "there's nothing we could steal!"

Eve knew of their desperate situation now, but Mrs. Oliver was still under the soothing impression that all was well; Keith working, Norah working, and Norah's employers so generous as to give her many afternoons off so that she might care for her mother.

"I wish it was spring, dear," her mother would say, "so that you and I could get out into the park!"

Norah would rouse herself from her magazine page drowsily.

"I like it here."

"You've grown so good, Nono, in these last few months. In that stuffy office all morning, and here taking care of me all afternoon. I remember, after Daddy died, all that you and Keith were going to do!" the invalid might muse on lovingly. "You were going to open a hotel, or raise fruit, or take children to tutor, or board old ladies. . . ."

Norah would listen with a sharp pang in her heart. Ah, those had been wonderful old days, when she and Keith, twenty-one and twenty-three, had indulged in wild dreams of success and achievement!

"And then last year too," her mother's gentle voice crooned on, one day, "only last year, just before we moved, David used to be in the house all the time, and I thought—we all thought, that something so happy was going to come of it!"

Norah's heart writhed with shame and pain as she listened. She made no comment.

The David affair had indeed commenced in happiness and confidence; everything was changed now, and she hated to remember it, hated to think of him. She had met him at one of the big football games at Princeton, just before her father's death; Norah had gone with a boy named Bunny Myers—she had not liked Bunny much, but any escort, rather than missing the game, had been acceptable, and Bunny had plenty of money, at least, and had led her, bundled up in Eve's new coat, and very pretty under a new brown hat, to excellent seats. And right behind them had been a party of four: two men and two girls, all old friends of Bunny's; Miss Porter and Miss Slade, and Mr. Thomas and Mr. Howard.

Ah, what a day that had been for Norah to remember, a day of crisp winter cold and the scent of violets; a day of growing excitement and triumph in her soul!

For David—he had only remained "Mr. Howard" for the first half of the game—had leaned over her shoulder, talked to her, laughed at her, showed in every way that he had been as much taken with Miss Oliver as Norah had felt herself to be with him. It had been instantaneous; thrilling and absorbing to them both. After all, the pretty Miss Slade he had taken to the game had proved to be his cousin, engaged to the great half-back they were all watching and cheering so enthusiastically; Norah had not been poaching on any other girl's preserves.

After the game they had all gone together to the Wilsons'. As far as Norah could ascertain at that time, or at any other, the Wilsons had no children, had no personal interest in the game. But they had had an enormous warm luxurious house near the ball field, and they had had fires and victrola music and big comfortable rooms and inexhaustible food; trays and trays of sandwiches and salads; fleets of smoking coffee cups and cakes. Some hundred young persons had been streaming about enjoying all this, and not the least had been Norah and David, ensconced in a stairway ingle behind palms, eating and drinking ravenously, laughing and talking eagerly, absorbed in the intoxicating emotions of that different kind of hunger and thirst that seems only to increase with the laughing encounter of eyes, the lowering of voices, the shy meeting of hands.

Bewilderedly, still together, they had sought out the Wilsons, at about eight o'clock, for grateful good-byes, and David had walked with Norah to her own house; the Olivers' pretty cottage not far from the college buildings. Here David had duly met her father in his invalid chair by the fire, and pretty little Eve, and Norah's mother. Her mother had been quite frankly aproned, quite honestly putting the last touches to an orderly kitchen; the Olivers had never been rich, and they made no pretenses.

Ah, yes, but that had been a pretty sort of poverty after all! It had been dignified, understandable; it had had nothing in common with the changes, the strange new order of things after Norah's father had died. The Olivers had come to New York then, to real poverty, the poverty of crowdedness and noise, of airshafts and house smells and angry neighboring voices, of shabbiness and weariness and discouragement.

For a while David had accepted all this cheerfully, loyally. He had brought Norah candy, discussed her first job sympathetically with her, taken her to movies. Late in his college work, because of years spent with his mother in Europe, David had been loitering through his sophomore grades; his car cost him more than Norah could earn. But he liked her, admired her, laughed at her; her changed fortunes made no difference to David Howard.

At first, that is. She knew exactly the day—almost the hour, when he had begun to feel the strain of their friendship; when richer girls, girls who chattered of cars and dances, trips and frocks and house parties, had begun to make their impression. She knew it increasingly; his absent-mindedness, his very kindness had told her.

And now, for months, she had had no word from him at all.

Chapter III

ON THE Saturday night that ended the anxious and disappointing week, she and Keith were reading in the sitting room after dinner; their mother was asleep.

The sitting room, while not entirely out of key with the shabbiness and darkness of the rest of the house, was nevertheless its brightest spot. There had been no room for the piano, which was in storage, but the big chairs were good, the lamps were softly colored and simple in design, and as many of the fine books of a happier day as could be squeezed in were aligned on shelves or piled on the table. The family's former grandeur was also indicated by the rich, stiff, gold-lined blue brocade of the window curtains, and although those windows commanded only a strip of crowded city street, their height, and the western skies they faced, insured them a flood of afternoon sunshine when there was sunshine at all.

Tonight the room was cosy with lamplight and furnace warmth. Norah had fallen into a sort of dream in her chair, and having secured, in her own imagination, an opportunity to take a small part in a forthcoming Broadway production, was in process of killing off the leading lady to afford herself a further chance, when Keith suddenly muttered "Damn!" under his breath.

His sister looked up, surprised, and at the sight of his anxious face her own grew sober.

"What's the matter, Keith?"

"Oh, nothing!" he said, as he had said a week ago. But this time his tone was different, and his expression did not indicate his old careless confidence.

"You and Anne haven't quarreled?"

"Oh, no. Nothing like that. It's only——" Keith said restlessly, "it's only that I'll be darned if I know quite how we're going to get out of this!"

Norah felt a first premonitory conviction that matters really were serious. If *Keith* were scared——!

"Well, Eve's salary will pay the rent," she suggested helpfully.

"Yes. But it's nice to eat," Keith offered. And they both laughed suddenly and reluctantly.

"Well," Norah presently said, feeling the better for the laugh, "we're not going to be *beaten*. We're as intelligent as most people, and we're healthy and young, and we are willing to work hard——"

"I know," Keith agreed, as she paused. "And I tell myself that we will work out of this—in three years it'll all be straightened out somehow. But the point is, how?"

"In three years I'll be twenty-seven," Norah mused.

"But what's that got to do with it?"

"Nothing," she said.

"Darn it," the boy said, "there's no one we could borrow from!"

"There are banks."

"You can't just go to a bank and ask for money."

"Not without securities, no."

They were both silent. Suddenly Keith said:

"The Howards have scads of money."

The blood rushed to Norah's face, and she looked at him almost fearfully.

"Keith, you wouldn't—we couldn't——"

"No, of course not!" he said hastily.

"We hardly know them," Norah stammered, not entirely reassured. "I only know David, and I don't know him any more!"

And again they were both silent, thinking.

"We've never gotten up against anything quite as hard as this before, have we, Keith?"

"No," he admitted, a little reluctantly.

"It sounds so—sensational," Norah began, and hesitated. "But Mother has that jewelry; she has her engagement ring."

Keith faintly shook his head.

"It wouldn't carry us two months."

"Well, then there's Bill Gunther," Norah suggested dubiously. Her brother's brow grew dark.

Bill Gunther had recently married their sister.

"I'll be—damned," Keith said firmly, "if I ever give that rotter a chance to patronize *us!* Anyway," he added, suddenly cooling, "he hasn't got anything. He has his job, and his father has money—that's all there is to that."

"What are loan societies, Keith?" Norah asked. Keith pondered this subject for a while, and then said without any particular enthusiasm that he would see about the loan societies on Monday.

And it was at breakfast on that very Monday that Eve said casually, amusedly:

"Listen, Norah—here's a girl in the paper who says she will marry any man who will take care of her invalid father!"

"Oh, no?" Norah said, feeling the room go around.

She reached for the paper: they had put her letter at the top of the column.

"I think it's silly, because she wouldn't, nobody would!" Eve said.

"You notice she doesn't put in her name," Keith commented.

"Ex-exactly," Norah managed to say unsteadily.

"What kind of a man would take up a proposition like that?" the younger sister observed, leaning against Norah's arm to reread the letter.

Norah, after a panicky glance that reassured

her as to her not having been, by any horrible chance, betrayed, thought that the phrases of the letter rolled along very well. They had misspelled the word "husband" by a typographical error; she felt all the author's agony at the disfigurement of her child, as she saw that it had been printed "hubsand." But neither Keith nor Eve seemed to notice the error: they were too much concerned in the idea.

"What kind of a man?" Keith repeated Eve's query. "Oh, a rotter of some sort, looking for a few evenings' fun, or blackmail, or for a chance to insure her and then murder her!"

"Oh, Keith, does it follow?" Norah asked, trying for an idle, natural voice.

"Well," the boy said, with a touch of the haughtiness that was characteristic of the Olivers, "I wouldn't want one of my sisters to get mixed up in any such business!"

"I should hope not!" Norah agreed dutifully, reading the letter again. She was fascinated by the sight of her own words actually in print, and all that day the dreary business of job-hunting was brightened by the thought of the various men, lonely men, who might see the "Open Forum" today and wish that they might get in touch with "Wife for Sale."

The next morning, printed in the same newspaper column, there were six or seven letters answering, condemning, or praising "Wife for

Sale," and a pathetic contribution from someone who described himself as a "young Swedish scholar," asserting that in seven months in the big city he had never found a real friend. Among the personals also Norah found three invitations addressed to "Wife for Sale."

It was so exciting to find herself even anonymously in the center of this controversy that she almost forgot the slowly accumulating discouragement of the winter days; the unwelcome approach of Christmas to a family that this year could not be sure of rent or warmth, much less turkey and presents and tree. There had never been a Christmas in the Oliver annals without a tree.

In the second week of December things came to a crisis. All of Norah's money was gone. Keith's was almost gone. Mrs. Oliver's doctor said encouragingly that she could go on now to a diet of broiled chicken, cream, chops, roast beef. "And after Christmas we must see about getting those delicate tubes of yours into the sunshine somewhere!" he said.

Keith got Christmas work in a mail-order house in New Jersey. Norah stayed home and took care of the silent, chilly, impoverished rooms and the invalid. Secretly she answered every one of the "Wife for Sale" advertisements, protecting her anonymity by means of a newspaper box.

Most of them, as Keith had predicted, only produced by way of response a crop of milliners' advertisements and the cards of fortune-tellers and matrimonial agencies. One or two were genuine answers, written in pencil on lined paper, misspelled and illiterate, yet somehow very touching in their loneliness and eagerness.

One she nearly missed. It was merest chance that took her eye down the short column of personals one morning, and arrested her attention at seven or eight closely packed lines that were signed *"Hubsand."*

"My dear," the advertisement began smoothly, *"if you really mean it and really can make your assertions good, why not try Princeton and Oxford? Any opportunity treated with greatest appreciation and respect. My offer extremely advantageous to all, please communicate at once with your devoted*

"Hubsand."

Norah studied the scrap of gray paper with a fast-beating heart. Was it an answer to "Wife for Sale," or was it only a coincidence? It might be some man advising his wife—say his divorced wife—about placing their son in school. Or "advantageous to all" might mean that this graduate of Princeton and Oxford was promising assistance to "Wife for Sale's" invalid father.

But if he really wanted to get in touch with

the writer of the letter, why hadn't he simply headed his personal as the others had done? Well—perhaps he had wanted to test her sharpness—perhaps he had been as half-hearted in responding to her call as she had been in sending it.

Anyway, she had been too keen eyed for him; his little ruse had failed. Norah read the personal again and felt quite sure that "Hubsand" was a rather conceited young fellow, pluming himself on that Princeton and Oxford record, and willing to patronize "Wife for Sale." For that matter, Keith had had his two years at Yale, and would have graduated with honors if Dad hadn't been ill.

A newspaper box number was given at the end of the notice; she wrote it down. All morning long, as she washed dishes and made beds, the phrasing of a note to "Hubsand" occupied her thoughts.

When she went out to market she mailed a prim, unsigned typewritten permission to him to address "Wife for Sale" at her newspaper box.

"What harm does it do?" she asked herself, as she went on to the hot little busy bakery and loitered through the big market. "I meet him, I talk to him, I don't like him. What of it?"

Her thoughts danced about him; she was bold, she was afraid, by turns. Keith came home that night all but despairing; Norah was only partially conscious of his distress.

"Guatemala," her brother muttered, when they were alone after dinner. Norah turned amazed from the dish-pan. Was he still harping upon Guatemala?

"How could you go now, Keith? We couldn't *all* go, on a hundred a month."

"It would probably be more than that," he murmured. And then, wretchedly, "I was thinking of Anne. Her people—her mother wants her to go abroad. They don't like me. They don't want her to think about me."

Norah's heart was sick with sympathy. Her vague dreams of "Hubsand" disappeared. While she had been feeding herself on this imaginary stuff, poor Keith was longing to be free, longing to be able to take his girl away with him.

"God has completely abandoned us," she thought, as she lay in bed that night. "There isn't any use struggling or worrying, we can't do anything. We'll just have to wait for our fate, whatever it is. Other people have ups and downs financially, they have comparative troubles. We're just—down and out, and nobody knows, and nobody's going to help us."

Chapter IV

A DOZEN hours later she had his letter in her hand: "Hubsand" had answered her! His name was Barry Dunsmuir—unless indeed he had chosen this romantic title as a disguise. But the letter did not sound romantic. It was typed on office paper; very handsome paper, and it was signed in a fine, compact, firm hand. The firm was Coates & Goldman, Electric Engineers, and engraved at the top was something that looked like a compass.

"Perhaps you will come and have luncheon with me on Friday, at one o'clock at the Chatham?" wrote Mr. Dunsmuir. *"I may have to leave town within a fortnight, and would appreciate a talk with you before I go. Please write me at my club, or telephone me at the office, if you decide to come."*

The Chatham: nothing could be safer than that. A conservative hotel with a famous cuisine, right downtown in the hotel district. And if he tried anything irregular, Norah thought, she would simply turn on her heel and leave him. After all, one was not quite a child!

Perhaps he did not want a wife at all; perhaps he was an old man who already had a nice old wife, and the wife wanted a social secretary. Norah saw herself writing letters, acknowledging flowers, answering the telephone for old Mrs. Dunsmuir.

At all events, matters at home were at so desperate a pass, the future was so dark, that she must make for any port in a storm. Mr. Dunsmuir could not hurt her, and if he really were a Princeton and Oxford man and a gentleman, he might help.

When she took the subway downtown and walked westward to Vanderbilt Avenue, Norah's purse was flat and almost empty. Within it were a silver quarter dollar, two dimes, and several pennies. She had spent her own last dollar days ago; this money was what remained from two dollars Keith had given her yesterday. She had said to him fearfully, "Keith, can you spare it?" and he had said, "Sure!" with all his usual confidence. But she knew his own money was running very low.

December sixteenth; shop windows were looped and crisscrossed with tinsel, and decorated with red stars and silver bells. Toys glittered red behind the steamed glass; revolving doors gave forth puffs of heated air; the world smelled of popcorn and evergreen.

Norah had made herself look her prettiest;

she did not know that excitement and trepidation were doing their part too, putting dark flames into her gray eyes and sending a fluctuating exquisite color to her clear, pale cheeks. She felt her heart almost suffocate her as she walked through a glass-paneled old oak doorway into the wide entrance hallway of the hotel and looked about her nervously without being able to see anything or anyone distinctly.

There was a subdued gloom here: emptiness, palms, walls paneled in dark wood. It was not like a hotel; it was like a club, like some old English corridor leading to galleries, ancestral halls. There were big leather chairs all about, most of them empty. Two women were murmuring on a wide leather davenport; a man was writing at an oak desk. A small dark scowling man, pale, and heavily spectacled—not a boy——

He looked up, nodded and smiled, got to his feet.

"I'm Barry Dunsmuir," he said immediately, taking her hand. "You're Miss——"

"Oliver," Norah supplied faintly. Something died out of her heart at that moment. A tall, broad-shouldered, athletic man—like David, only not fair—vanished from her dreams as if he had never been. This—this—this sick-looking, eyeglassed, grinning man—— Well, she must be polite.

"I have a table," Mr. Dunsmuir said, leading the way to the dining room. They were placed by the window, inconspicuous, unobserved, and she sat down, in a sort of vertigo of disappointment and shame, laid her gloves beside her plate, and kept her eyes fixed seriously on his.

"What do you like, Miss Oliver? I'm having pea soup because I happen to have a weakness for pea soup. Would you rather have oysters than pea soup? And afterward their special chicken?"

He gave his order smartly, sharply; everything he did was done smartly and sharply. And when he had finished he crossed his arms on the table before him, and grinned at her engagingly, as if he were inviting her approval of his smartness and sharpness.

"Well," he said, "now we can talk. You know my name. What's yours?"

She took a card from her purse; laid it before him.

"Norah Ralston Oliver," he read. He glanced up. "It's a lovely name. I like it!"

And he emitted a chuckle that she afterward characterized to herself as elfin. He was rather like a satyr—or Pan—or a hobgoblin.

"Tell me about yourself," he was saying. "I want to know about you—your history. You've no relatives, no family except your father?"

Norah, disarmed, flushed and stammered; her

gray eyes guilty, her wide sweet young mouth apologetic.

"Well, that was partly made up," she explained, "to—to baffle the British police."

"To—what?"

"Oh, that's what we say—that was in *Captain Applejack*," the girl said, laughing confusedly and nervously. "Don't you remember he changed his name from Applejohn to Applejack, 'to baffle the British police'?"

"I had forgotten," the man said, watching her.

"We say that, in the family, whenever anyone lies about anything."

"There's a family, then?"

"My mother and two sisters and my brother Keith."

"Oh, Lord!" Barry Dunsmuir ejaculated involuntarily.

"But my sister Elinor is married—she was married quite suddenly last year. Mother didn't like the way they did it—her going off with Mr. Gunther, and so we don't see her very much. They live in a little apartment on East Sixty-seventh."

"And why did your mother disapprove?"

He had a quick, almost pouncing manner; it was as if, she thought afterward, he was filling out a blank, and she under cross-examination.

"Well, Mr. Gunther had been married before

WIFE FOR SALE

and divorced. My sister—she's very pretty—was his secretary. Mother didn't—like it."

"And what," the man asked, with a chuckle that brought the annoyed color to her face, "what does Mother think of this performance of yours?"

"She has no idea of it."

"I see."

"She'd think it was—simply disgraceful," Norah added, beginning herself to think it was rather disgraceful.

"Nothing disgraceful about it!" he said briskly.

"So far!" she agreed, with a sudden flash of spirit. They both laughed.

"Nothing disgraceful at all," he persisted. "You want a protector, a position, and I—*happen* to want a wife."

Norah's face was scarlet; she could not speak.

"It's been going on for a long, long time," Barry said. "It's arranged that way in the most civilized communities of the world. The French, the Chinese, the Spanish, the Jews, they all pick out suitable mates for their children, and make the arrangements. The man gives so much—protection, position, support—and the woman on her side gives so much too. Why not? That's the way the world moves."

"I can't say that I thought it out that far," Norah confessed, finding at last a chance to speak. "It was—I'm ashamed to say, a joke. I *was* worried—my mother *is* ill, and my brother Keith has lost his job, and I lost mine——"

And suddenly, to her own acute shame and self-contempt, she was crying bitterly and trying to stem the tide of tears with gulps of icewater and a determined stiffening of her jaw.

"I don't know why I'm so silly!" she presently could say thickly. "I'm t-t-tired, I guess. I was up with Mother in the night. And everything—everything seems so—so *puzzling*. I didn't know what to do!"

Grinning his odd grin, watching her with alert attention, Barry Dunsmuir began to talk. If it was done to cover her little breakdown it displayed no particular sympathy; the waiter had brought the soup, and as its heat began to restore Norah to self-control, she became aware that the man was telling her his own history in turn.

"I had my own hard time, too," he was saying, in his sharp, dry fashion. "There was lots of money when I was a kid, and my father sent me to Princeton and afterward for a year in England. My mother died when I was ten—that was a good many years ago, and when I was just twenty-one my father married again. After that something happened to the family business—the textile business, incidentally, and when he died three years ago he only left some insurance for the widow.

"I'm an explorer—did I write you that in my note?"

"An *explorer?*"

"Yes. I've been on two expeditions with Sassoon, and on some shorter trips. Ten years ago I was engaged to be married to an English girl —she was very delicate, died in Palermo two years later; they had taken her there for the winter. After that I went off on trips with research men, and last year with Sassoon. Did you ever hear him talk?"

"No, but he must be very interesting," Norah said politely, trying to think what he did. Her eyes were dry now, and she had blown her nose, and felt composed again. She must look like a fright, but it didn't matter.

"He's a king," Barry said, as if to himself. "He's going off to the South Pole now—down to Ross Bay and all the Scott country. God, what a trip!"

"And are you going with him?"

"No such luck. I've not got the eyes. He's going to be gone ten months; starts in about three weeks. But don't you read the papers?" He was pouncing again. "Haven't you been following it?"

"I read the papers, of course. But not that sort of thing."

"Well, let's get down to business," Barry said. Norah's heart turned over, and she felt a little chill ripple from her heels to the roots of her hair.

"Just one minute, Mr. Dunsmuir," she said quickly. "Let me say this first. It was a silly thing I did, writing that letter—I didn't mean it! I've been horribly ashamed of it since. Of course I couldn't—seriously—have considered for one instant—no girl would——"

She stopped, smiling nervously, looking at him appealingly.

"Well, I rather thought you would back out of it," the man said, with his unearthly grimace and chuckle. He shrugged. "That's up to you, of course," he conceded, in an indifferent tone.

"I feel horribly—flat about it," said Norah. "I hope you won't think I wanted a husband badly enough to—to advertise in the newspapers for one. I don't know what I was thinking about when I wrote that silly letter!"

"Well, I want a wife!" Barry admitted, and laughed. His laugh was simply ghoulish, Norah decided.

"You must know girls—women—you would rather marry, than a person you never have seen," she suggested politely, uncomfortably.

"I don't," he said. "I know some women who might try it. But they aren't what I want. In fact," he said, and Norah was interested in spite of the fact that he roused in her somehow a feeling of antagonism, "in fact, I didn't know that what I wanted was a wife until I read your letter.

"My life is funny, you see. I'm either away on these research expeditions, or I'm shut up in a laboratory or study working on my notes. I've got the material for a book ready—a textbook on South Sea fungi. There's a year's work on it, and I've got to live somewhere and eat while I'm working.

"When I got back two months ago—back from this trip with Sassoon, d'you see?—I found that my father's brother had left me some money and a place in northern New Jersey. That's where I'm going to do my book and have my laboratory. I'll have to have a couple of servants there —there are cows, horses—I've not seen the place for years, but I remember it. Foxaway, in New Jersey—that's its name. It's the one place in the world I've always wanted to live!

"It occurred to me just last week that if there was a woman who wanted that sort of thing— garden, sunshine, whatnot for her sick father— or, as it turns out, her sick mother—we might strike a bargain. You run the place and the meals and be company for me—she sits out in the sun and gets well—I write my book and pay bills."

A silence. He was grinning at her behind the strong glasses with a half impish, half expectant smile on his pale, intellectual face.

"You didn't know, you see," Norah said, by

way of answer, "that I had a nineteen-year-old sister, Eve, and a mother and brother, and another sister, married—and my uncle Rodney."

"I didn't hear about Uncle Rodney!"

"He's my mother's uncle. He never does anything much," Norah explained innocently, "and when we had it, we always gave him money—a little, and asked him to dinner when he came. I don't know how he lives, really."

"Your brother wanted to get married, you said."

"Well, he does, yes. His girl's family is quite rich, and they think Keith isn't good enough for her, and it worries him. He'd like to take a job in Guatemala, only he's needed at home."

"You and your mother and sister can't get along without him?"

"Just now we can't!" she admitted proudly, reluctantly.

"If you married you could snap your fingers at him."

Norah thought of handsome, dark, vivid Keith, his affection, his laughter, his courage.

"I don't want to snap my fingers at him."

"And the sister, couldn't she live with the married sister?"

Norah made no answer. Her earnest face with its dark lashes, with the straight clean line of her nose and the generous sweetness of her red mouth, was darkened by a faint scowl. Bright tendrils of her hair curved against the line of her smart, shabby little hat; there were pearls in her ears. Her eyes were absent; she had forgotten her companion.

"I've thought of everything; it's no use," she burst out, in a low, rebellious voice. "I've thought of dressmaking and manicuring and teaching! You have to have regular courses for all of them; I can't afford the time. I'd be a nurse, except for Mother. I'd open a hotel or a restaurant, but you have to have space. You have to have backing to open a school—gymnasiums and French teachers. You can't make jam on a four-burner gas stove, or bake cake in an oven one foot square. I've applied to dentists and to interior decorators and professional shoppers—nobody wants anybody this year.

"Of course," she added, after a pause long enough to give her time to be ashamed of her emotion, "of course I'll get a job, and it won't be waitress or chambermaid, either. There *are* jobs, thousands of them, and there *are* girls getting married and stopping work. In the five-and-ten last week the woman told me——"

Barry interrupted her, or rather spoke as she stopped for breath.

"Mightn't your job with me be your best bet? Mind you, it wouldn't be all fun. You'd have your mother with you, yes, and no money trouble, and you'd be able to help your uncle and let your brother get married. But it'd be terribly lonely for you—gardening, reading Shakespeare—no matinées and beauty parlors, no parties. How old are you?" he broke off to ask.

"Twenty-four," she answered in a surprised tone. Her letter had said that.

"I know you said you were twenty-four. But I expected a woman much older. I don't ask you to decide today," the man said. "I couldn't decide myself, today. But why not carry this venture a little further? Why not lunch together every day for a week, and then decide? I've been realizing this last week that I want a wife—no, not you especially, Norah, you don't have to get so red!—but woman—as woman. D'you see? I want companionship. I like someone with me at dinner, and in the evenings, and in my room. I get lonely in the night. She might talk to me about her clothes, and the letters she got from her sisters. I—I'd like it."

Norah's color was flaming again. She laughed a little uncomfortably.

"I don't see," she protested lightly, "how any man could ever like, ever respect, a woman he met through a newspaper advertisement! It's cold-blooded. It's too businesslike."

"Oh, come now." It was the satyr at his superior worst. "How about royalty, the nobility? That's the way they manage it."

"I haven't much use for the nobility, or royalty either!" the girl countered quickly.

"But socially they're accepted," Barry answered, as quickly as she. "They bargain," he said, "they quibble and haggle for months. And then the Princess is informed of her fate."

"It's barbaric!" Norah said, trying to laugh.

"I don't know. The other way doesn't always work any too well, either."

There was a silence. Their lunch was over. They walked to the door of the hotel, and Norah, already reflecting that she must expend another nickel on the trip home, held out her hand in farewell.

"Lunch with me here, tomorrow?" the man said. "If you're job-hunting, you'll be in this neighborhood somewhere. I might hear of a job. It will do no harm to lunch together again."

The girl hesitated. She had forty-eight cents in her purse. There was food in the apartment for perhaps two days, and Keith had less than ten dollars in the world. Mother was still weak and helpless; Eve growing restive and angry under the strain that was so much too serious for her nineteen years.

She glanced at her companion, gloved now, with his fur-collared overcoat belted around him, and his glasses flashing under the sober winter sky. He wanted a wife, this man—at his dinner table, in his room, in his arms at night.

He had said so. And she could not—she could not go on with all this much longer!

But she dared not hesitate.

"All right; I'll be here!" she said.

"Good!" Barry approved. He turned sharply on his heel; gave her a last keen look and an unsmiling nod; walked away.

Chapter V

NORAH found herself trembling. Vaguely, not knowing where she was going, she started eastward; turned back, walked irresolutely toward the north. She could take the subway anywhere; she must get rid of this nervous burning in her cheeks, this uncomfortable pressure at her heart.

What was she doing? To what was she pledging herself? Had she departed from her senses?

East Sixty-sixth. Norah's heart beat faster; this was David's street. She walked slowly along toward the park; looking for the number. She had come to this house once for a Sunday lunch, and had gone afterward to a movie with David. It had been a great occasion, an exciting occasion in anticipation, but not a happy time in fact. There had been smart girls and men at the lunch, all with plans. They had been going to Patsy's, and then on to the rehearsal at Jean's. They had not said that they wanted David with them, but Norah had known it as clearly from their manner as any words could have made it; David had wanted to go with them, she had seen that, too. It had not been particularly thrilling for him to leave them all chattering and laughing intimately, and take his own girl, a stranger to them, a girl who didn't belong, to a movie. Anyone could go to a movie; mighty few men were lucky enough to be wanted at Patsy's house and at Jean's. But of course Norah hadn't been known by either girl, hadn't been asked to the delights of the rehearsal—he couldn't take her very well.

She remembered the miseries of the movie; her impulse to tell him to leave her there and go back to his own people, her impulse toward tears. A wretched failure of a day, made no easier by the sympathetic enthusiasm of her mother and Eve afterward, when they had cross-examined her happily and proudly; what had the Howard home been like? Patricia Hunter—oh, her name was always in the social columns! Jean Haverstock was the girl who won all the horse-show prizes, wasn't she?

Today, somberly inspecting the outside of the magnificent Howard mansion, tired, puzzled, excited, Norah remembered that Sunday. Ah, why couldn't the Howard heir be the spectacled, cackling little man she had just left, and her "want-ad" husband be David, big and square and tawny-headed, superbly sure of himself! David was only a few months older than herself; this Dunsmuir man was her senior by almost eleven years.

Why couldn't David emerge from his house

now, in his big warm coat, and see her, and cross the narrow street with his eager heartening laugh, and take her to tea somewhere; some softly lighted, scented, music-drowned place where they could murmur and smile at each other, unobserved, and where the sting of these wretched months of silence could be all wiped away?

"Oh, David, come out—come out—come out!"

David, fifty miles away, taking a chemistry test, naturally did not come out. Norah loitered past the house with a sick, discouraged feeling in her heart; turned and loitered back again. The Howard house remained unresponsive; its fine windows were heavily draped and shaded; no one came or went on the handsome brownstone steps. From where she stood Norah could not have sworn that the place was tenanted at all; whatever life was there went on deep in the silence and richness of the carpeted and warmed and silent rooms, or in the obscurity of the servants' quarters.

The Bronx, by contrast with this elegance and reserve, smote upon her senses with a shock. Cold, bleak, dirty, the familiar corners, the familiar market with its frosted windows crowded with cheaply printed signs, the familiar smells and sounds of the hallway of her own house, were so many separate affronts.

"Hello, Mother darling! Should you be up?"

"Hello, dear. I've been peacefully sitting here peeling apples for a pie—I feel splendid. How was the office today?"

"The——? Oh, the office? Oh, just as usual."

"Dark, dreary weather, Norah."

"Tastes like snow. And a storm would be a sort of relief."

"Did you have any lunch, dear?"

"Oh, yes!" Norah was conscious of a laugh, deep down inside her. She had had the famous pea soup, delicious chicken with mushrooms, peas, a delicate salad; she had had a meringue glacé and coffee—not for many months had Norah Oliver enjoyed a meal like that!

Or had she enjoyed it? Had she been too nervous, too much excited to enjoy it? Her thought went back to Barry Dunsmuir: "The little gadfly!" she said, half aloud.

"What did you say, dear?"

Norah turned from the closet where she had been hanging her coat.

"Thinking aloud, Mother."

"Norah, sit down here for a moment. Are you worried about anything?" her mother asked simply.

Color crept up under the girl's pale clear skin.

"Worried, darling?"

"Keith has lost his job," Mrs. Oliver said simply.

Norah made an effort at naturalness.

"Keith has?"

"I'm sure of it. Twice now," the older woman went on, "I've telephoned him during office hours. They didn't *say* he had left, but there was something extremely queer in the way the telephone girl answered me! Do you know anything about it?"

"I think he feels—he suspects that they won't want him after Christmas," Norah admitted guardedly.

"But *your* job is all right, Norah!" It was an exclamation of fear and appeal, rather than a question. Norah smiled.

"You know me, Mother."

"I know you're extremely valuable to them!" Mrs. Oliver said, reassured. "But, Norah, what are we to do about Keith?" she resumed anxiously.

"He's looking for another job. He'll get one!"

"Oh, dear, dear, dear!" her mother wailed, smiting her palms together. "It does seem as if everything came at once. My illness—I'm still so wretchedly weak. My knees almost failed me when I walked just this far into the kitchen, today, and if anything happens to Keith's job I really don't know *what* we will do! Before, I had my insurance, you know—that's gone now."

"Darling, you're still weak and sick, or you wouldn't let it frighten you so," Norah soothed her, one arm about the thin shoulders, her young cheek against her mother's faded one. "We'll get out of it all. Thousands of other families are worse off than we are this winter! Keith," Norah went on boldly, "isn't in the least alarmed! Why, he's got a very good job offered him, right now, only it's down in Madagascar or Guatemala or somewhere, and he doesn't want to leave home!"

"Oh, Norah, you're such a comfort to me!" her mother said, leaning her head against Norah's shoulder.

"You're such a scare-cat!" Norah countered in loving reproof. But in her heart she was afraid.

That Sunday her mother was well enough to go to church with Eve. Norah was left alone in the apartment; it occurred to her as she made beds and wiped dishes that David might be at home—might even be alone and lonely, too. She did not wait to think about it; she went at once to the telephone.

No need to look up his number; she had it always in her mind. Was Mr. David Howard there? Yes, Matam, I believe so, Matam, said the voice of the English butler cordially. David's voice came ringing over the line a minute later, full of vigor and pleasure.

"Hello, Gladys! Prompt to the second. I told Collins that you'd call."

"But this isn't Gladys, whoever Gladys is!" Norah told him gayly, over a horrible sinking at her heart. "This is Norah."

"Norah?"

"Yes, Norah Oliver."

A pause.

"Oh, hello, Norah, how's everything with you?" David said then flatly. All the enthusiasm had departed from his tone.

They talked for perhaps two minutes. David said that he had been thinking about her, he was terribly busy. Norah asked him forced, pleasant questions to which she already knew the answers: he graduated this June, didn't he? And were they going abroad again?

She hung up the telephone, her face blazing. He had made no overtures, suggested no engagement. He had known that she wanted to get in touch with him; it had made no difference in his full and happy plans.

For a long time after the telephone conversation was concluded Norah sat perfectly still in the empty kitchen, staring stonily into space. After a while she spoke aloud.

"Well, Barry, I guess you win!" she said.

Chapter VI

SHE had to be honest with him. Indeed, there was small chance of being anything else under those sharp piercing eyes.

"It's because you—annoy me!" she said.

"Annoy you?"

"Yes. You—you make me feel all prickly. I want to—to yell, 'Oh, shut up!' at you," confessed Norah.

He laughed delightedly.

"What? When I talk?"

"Yes; almost always. Not always. But almost always when you say things—you make me mad," Norah said, with youthful simplicity.

"What do I say that makes you mad?"

"It's the way you say it—say everything!"

"Why, you often get the better of me in argument," Barry said, baiting her.

"I *never* get the better of you! I don't even know the *names*," Norah said almost reproachfully, "of the things you talk about all the time—Russian schools, and bugs, and the climate of the antarctic, and who was responsible for the war, and fungus!"

"Come, you said that Russia sounded crazy

to you, without any homes or any religion, and I was very much impressed."

"Well, I got that out of the paper."

Barry said, after a silence through which he had smiled at her his disquieting smile,

"Suppose your husband did happen to know more of world politics than you do. What of it?"

"I wouldn't want to marry anyone who was laughing at me," Norah said, flushed and smiling and nervous, but speaking steadily. "I've—liked lots of men less than I like you," she added placatingly, "and I'd marry them in a minute! But I couldn't—I couldn't marry anyone who might be laughing at me, even then, when we were married, about—about being married! You've been terribly kind to me," she concluded, stammering a little in her anxiety to save his feelings, "and I've enjoyed these lunches. When you talk about things it interests me, and I think that I'll study them up some day—and maybe I will, too. When you talked German to the waiter I wanted—terribly to understand. But I don't feel as if I understood *you* very well."

Barry was silent, looking at her, and after a pause she added, somewhat lamely, "Perhaps you feel the same way I do about it. Perhaps you feel that you—like me, and all that, but that you simply couldn't marry me!"

"No, I don't feel that way at all," he said, with

a little spurt of laughter. "I think we ought to go through with our contract."

"We didn't have any contract!"

"No, but you stated that you would marry anyone who met certain conditions, Norah. Now I've met them, or I've expressed a perfect willingness to meet them. I've got a country house that would offer perfect conditions for your mother's recovery; I've got money enough; you know enough about me to know that I'm not going to spring another wife on you, or blackmail you, or murder you. That was what your brother feared, wasn't it? I took you down to my offices and introduced you to old Judge Bailey, who was best man at my father's wedding; you met my partners there.

"Now I know that circumstances haven't improved much with you——"

He stopped on an interrogative note, with an upward glance, and Norah's rueful laugh conceded that circumstances had changed only for the worse.

"And now," Barry summarized it, "you don't want to get married at all."

"Well, marriage is—different when you come right up against it, Mr. Dunsmuir."

"Different from what?"

"From business. Marriage really is—ought to be, romantic and thrilling and—oh, everything," floundered Norah. "There's no use trying to manage it any other way."

There was another silence, and she tried to go on quite naturally with her tea; they were having tea together on Christmas Eve. They had lunched or had tea together every day for eight days now, talking of anything and everything without restraint, but Barry had faced the situation quite honestly today, and had asked her how she felt about marrying him.

Norah had attempted raillery, "Oh, you don't *have* to ask me that!" But she had been quickly sobered, and an uncomfortable and increasingly frank talk had followed.

She liked him, she had said with a little difficulty, but he made her "mad," he made her feel "all prickly." He was always laughing at her. She knew she was stupid about lots of things, but it was only when she was with Mr. Dunsmuir that she—well, *minded* it.

Now he was silent, and Norah could think of nothing to say; she wondered how she was ever going to end this hour, and whether she would ever see him again after it.

"You see, Norah," he said suddenly, in an odd tone, "this hasn't gone according to schedule."

"Hasn't?" she faltered, with an anxious frown.

"Not exactly!" Barry admitted, with his uncanny chuckle. "I've gotten in deeper than I meant to; I want to go through with it."

Norah hooked her two thumbs on the table; looked down at them. Her face was red.

"Well, thank you!" she said uneasily, clearing her throat.

"You'd like Foxaway," Barry suggested. "It's a grand old place—it's the only place in the world——" He stopped.

"I was going to say," he presently recommenced, "that it's the only place in the world I ever wanted to live in. I'd like to live there. The family's been there for two hundred years.

"I've got a cousin, Hazel Dunsmuir, who wanted it. She's got everything else in the world, but she wanted Foxaway. She told me so, asked me to write a new will and leave it to her. I thought—" he was laughing again—"I thought she had a cheek!"

"I should think *she* would be a good person for you to marry," Norah suggested. He gave her a quick glance.

"Hazel? Great Scott!" he ejaculated. "No," he added, in a ruminating tone, "I'll not marry Hazel, nor her dear friend Lucile. Nope. But the more I think of this bargain of ours, Norah," he concluded, brightening, "the better I like it! You run Foxaway, and take care of me——"

She looked at him with a timid, puzzled expression.

"Would there be any chance of its coming out right, do you suppose?" she asked.

"Every chance!" he answered encouragingly. "We're sensible people, you and I. We respect each other, we like each other. You aren't afraid of the country, or loneliness, or managing a farm."

He stopped on a quizzical little look, with his baffling laugh, but Norah was serious.

"Oh, no, that part would be all right!" she said, brushing it aside carelessly. "The only thing—the thing is——"

"What? What are you trying to say?"

"You're so quick," she murmured, frowning faintly, narrowing her eyes as she looked into space. "You always—make me feel as if you were laughing at me. But—but what I meant was—I wouldn't——"

"Wouldn't what?" he took her up briskly.

"Well, I wouldn't want to go into it unless we felt, we both felt, that there was a reasonable chance that it *would* work out. That you'd do your book, and I'd run the farm, and—we'd like each other—go on liking each other."

"We have as good a chance as anyone!" Barry offered.

"You don't," she said, suddenly steady and dignified, "love me."

His chuckle had in it a delighted note.

"And you don't love me!"

"No," Norah agreed, looking at him thoughtfully, "I don't. So oughtn't that—to settle it—end it?"

"On the contrary," he answered promptly, "that's exactly what ought to—begin it. That's exactly what we propose to do, marry because you can do a great deal for me, and I can solve some problems for you. It's *exactly* as it should be! I like you, I respect you, you're a gentlewoman. That's all. As for losing sleep and writing love letters—those things don't count, anyway."

Norah looked down at her thumbs again, thinking.

"I wish I knew what to do!" she said presently, looking up. "Suppose you weren't happy after we were married? Suppose you didn't like having my mother up at the farm?"

"Then I could get out."

She was never conscious of liking him, even when he was gentle and serious like this, but at such moments she felt a rush of pity, of kindliness for him.

"How could you get out, with your book not finished, and everything?"

"You see what a good wife you'd make me, Norah, already thinking about my book!"

"Oh, well," she said, shrugging and flushing. If he was going to be annoying again! Wife, indeed!

"It would be to get rid of all your other

troubles at once," he said. "You'd have—me instead. You'd have new ones, but they mightn't be so bad."

"I've always thought I could make a success of anything," Norah began slowly, after troubled thought. "I've always felt that I could—succeed. But I don't know about succeeding at this. It all began so queerly."

"It might have begun quite normally. Our finding each other as we did isn't important. We might have been introduced by anybody. I might have been in your office. You might have been my secretary."

"I know."

"This would be my plan," he said. "You and I get married tomorrow—no, dash it, tomorrow's Christmas, isn't it? I hate Christmas. We get married——"

"You hate Christmas!"

"Oh, yes," he said impatiently, carelessly, "it seems to me the bunk! But the day after Christmas——"

"But don't you—don't you believe in *God?*" Norah exclaimed.

"I believe in a great many gods, all of whom have done their feeble best to help humanity in one way or another. Prophets, doctors, scientists, they're all gods."

"They are not!" Norah protested sharply.

"Aren't they? Well, I'd leave that to you. At

any rate, you might believe what you liked—
that's one part of what I believe. And perhaps
you'd convert me, Norah."

"No, I'd never convert you," she said sadly.

"Why not?"

"Because, to convert a person——" Norah
stopped short. "I don't know exactly how to say
it," she said hesitatingly. "But faith—believing,
isn't a matter of—statistics. And you—you're all
for statistics. You'd believe in God if He could
be proved on a table of weights or something
out of a book."

"Well, and shouldn't He be?"

"Not that way."

"What way, then? By a lot of hysterical
mystics with visions and miracles?"

"No," she said steadily. "But not by—by facts,
either."

"Oh, come now! If a theory won't stand
analysis——!"

"Nothing worth while will stand analysis,"
Norah persisted. "You're laughing at me again;
I know how smart you are! But if you could
analyze Him and understand Him, He wouldn't
be God. He'd be something *you* did, not—not
what He is.

"You can't do that with anything worth
while," she went on, as Barry, watching her
curiously, was silent. "The way you feel about—
well, when it's spring, and the florists' awnings

are out again, and there are cherries. Or the way a person loves a baby. Or even the way you might love a dog. There's no reason in it, and no science, and no statistics. You have to—to wait for it, and feel it in your soul."

"And that's better than reason, is it?"

"That," she said seriously, "is the Holy Spirit."

"And how—" his voice was bantering, as usual, but his expression, for once, was not mischievous, "how do you—invite—encourage—discover the Holy Spirit?"

Norah looked puzzled, looked away, frowning slightly.

"Ask and you shall receive, I suppose," she answered, in a low, doubtful voice. Her cheeks were red.

"All of which," Barry presently said briskly, "brings us back to first principles. This is my idea. You and I get married day after tomorrow, and I—I take care of your immediate financial difficulties. On the twenty-eighth I leave with Sassoon—I'm going on the first lap with him; I'll come back on the escort ship. He goes to Hobart, ships a lot of equipment there, and goes on as soon as the ice breaks. I come back, and find you established in the New Jersey house, with your mother and your sister and anyone else you like—your uncle—I don't care. I pack all my stuff here, notes and specimens and typewriter and all that, and come up—say about March first. You and I tell them, then, that we're married, and in two weeks everything is running smoothly and comfortably, your mother is better, I'm settled down to work, and everything is fine."

"And what am I to tell them in the meanwhile?"

"What you like. Tell them that I am a scientist —an explorer, who wants a secretary-housekeeper."

During the desultory conversation they had finished their tea and had reached the foyer of the hotel on their way to the street. Norah, pulling on her shabby gloves, looked up at him in sudden timid hope.

"You don't want—just that? I mean a secretary and housekeeper, Mr. Dunsmuir?"

"Was it so nominated in the bond?"

"No," she admitted hesitatingly.

"I happen to like it best the other way," he said. "I like the spirit of a girl who could make such a proposition. I like—suddenly, the idea of a wife. I don't want to—to worry about you. I want you—*there,* belonging there, not thinking about running off elsewhere, or throwing up the job. And I want—well," he finished simply, "a wife."

Chapter VII

THEY were walking up the coid, dull street now; the sky was low and leaden; Christmas horns already were blowing.

"It's up to you," Barry resumed. "I don't say it's all roses for you: it's a job. I work hard, and I'm not especially sociable when I work. I hate the city, and there wouldn't be much theater and restaurant excitement in it for you. Of course, when I was off on a trip, you and your sister, your mother, could come down here, stay at a hotel, buy dresses—whatever women like to do. And when my book's finished I'm going to London for a year—six months, anyway, to work in the Geographical Society, and the museums and libraries: you might like that. But I don't say it's any snap for you, Norah.

"Meet me for lunch at—well, the Brevoort, on the day after tomorrow, and we'll go be married at the City Hall."

"My mother would think that was no marriage at all."

"All right, then, anywhere you say. And meanwhile—" they were turning into a big, bright bookshop—"meanwhile I have to give you a Christmas present, since you believe in Santa Claus," he said.

Norah watched him select a fat book; he took an envelope from his pocket just before the salesman wrapped it, and put it among the pages.

"That's a very small extra present, Norah," he said. "Let me do it! I know you want to buy your mother something—I know just how hard up you are."

Her face blazed. She put out a restraining hand.

"Please!" he said, chuckling, even though obviously in earnest. "Just as a friend. Not because I hope that you and your expenses are going to be up to me for life. But because I've got too much and you've got too little. Take it, for heaven's sake, and don't ever think of it again.

"And now for a final word," he went on, when they were in the street again. "We get married on Thursday. You go your way and I mine. You tell your mother whatever you like, and you and she move up to New Jersey. I'll put some money in the bank for you and go off with Sassoon. My uncle's estate isn't much—it's not settled yet, but it's something. When I get back, it will be all settled, and we'll make the announcement, and everything will be fine.

"Your brother, meanwhile, will probably have gone to Guatemala with his new wife. Your sister can do just as she likes. The first thing I'll do is fix your mother's affairs so that you needn't worry about her again: *that* was nominated in the bond, at least, and so you'll get what you want, and I'll get what I want, and everyone will be satisfied."

"But wouldn't that—Mother, I mean—take a terrible lot of money?"

"No—an annuity, something of that sort. The truth is, Norah," Barry said, "I haven't got so much money. I'll tell you all about it any time you care to listen. I've a small income, and I've the lump sum my uncle left me and the farm—there's a tenant farmer on it now, Taft, who pays me rent—and of course my book will make money: it may easily become the textbook, the reference book, on its subject. It's enough, but it isn't anything sensational."

"If it was ten dollars it would be more than the Oliver family has got at this moment," Norah said. Barry laughed.

"Before I get back you'll have time to get used to the place," he went on, after a moment. "There's a housekeeper there, an old crone named Huldy: she must be two hundred. I'll wire her before I go to have it all warmed up and get some groceries in."

It sounded adventurous, deliciously new and exciting. Norah's eyes were dancing as she faced him.

"I ought not to keep all this from my mother; but she's so weak, and she doesn't know you...."

"Meet me for lunch day after tomorrow," he said, at the subway hood. "And—oh, yes, Merry Christmas, Norah!"

"Merry Christmas!" she said.

In the hot, bright, tinsel and poinsettia draped bakery, a few minutes later, Norah opened her book and took out the envelope Barry had inserted in it. Five clean new twenty-dollar bills were in her hand. . . .

It took her breath away; she felt a little dizzy.

For a while she stood thinking, the money safe in her purse, her heart beating fast, her eyes shining.

Then she crossed the grimy frozen street to the market and stopped at the cashier's desk. The Olivers' butcher bill, please—and the grocery bill. They were not large: two of the crisp bills settled them once and for all.

Norah bought a turkey, a large limp turkey; cranberries, sweet potatoes, celery, a canned plum pudding. She went out to the street again on dancing feet and into one of the big department stores at the corner. Silk stockings for Eve, and socks for Keith, and a great fluffy new blanket in two tones of brown for Mother. No more piling of coats on Mother's feet on cold nights. A new alarm clock for Keith, whose old one had lately developed a tendency to ooze little screws and bolts; and fur-lined gloves for Eve——

And then she must stop. But her money was by no means gone; there was a twenty left, and a ten, and small money. Oh, it was delicious to have money, and now that she was miles away from Barry Dunsmuir she could like him, she could feel appreciative affection toward him, who was doing so much for her. It was only when she was with him that it was hard to think of herself as actually married to him.

A begging woman stopped her in the street; Norah gave her a dollar. "Oh, God bless you, my dear child!" the hoarse old voice said amazedly. Norah laughed, going on her way. She stopped at the five-and-ten, and bought two red paper wreaths for the front windows, and four red candles for the Christmas table. And, in the street again, she got her mother a bunch of violets for fifteen cents.

She carried these violets into the sick-room a little later. Keith was there, just a bulky shadow in the gloom; Norah set the flowers down and lighted a lamp.

"Look here, darling, these are your Christmas flowers!"

Mrs. Oliver looked pale and weak against her propping of pillows. There were tears in her eyes; she stretched her hand toward Norah.

"My darling, my brave dear children," she faltered. "I've just been hearing about it!"

"About what?" Norah said cheerfully, sitting down and putting her hand over her mother's reassuringly.

"About all you darlings—you *darlings* have been enduring, have been keeping from me," the mother said. "Keith's losing his job, you losing yours, both of you worried out of your wits, with your money getting shorter and shorter! Children, children, there was no need for all that. I'm well again, I can help."

"You could dig post holes for the new elevated," Norah suggested.

"Ah, no, dear, it's not funny! It makes me so proud, and yet it breaks my heart to think how different it all would have been if poor Daddy—— Norah, you should have told Mother, darling, it wasn't right to carry the whole load in your poor little heart!"

"Why'd you tell her?" Norah reproached her brother.

"Because I wanted to hock her emerald in the good old way," Keith said cheerfully. "And because I think I'll have to take up this Guatemala thing. They've promised me a raise in six months; I get my trip, of course. I might be able to help from there. I can't do anything here."

"Well, I'll tell you some good news, darlings," Norah said suddenly. Her face was very pale, but her eyes sparkled. "Eve!" she called, hearing her sister enter the kitchen. "Come in here and hear some news!"

"It's awful out," Eve said, shuddering with returning warmth as she came into the bedroom. "Hello, Mother dear. I'm dead. The rush today has been something ghastly. I'm going to stay in bed all day Christmas!"

"Mother knows about our jobs," Keith said sententiously.

"Well——" Eve said, shrugging. She turned fretfully to Norah. "Did Mrs. Flynn clean here yesterday or didn't she?" she demanded. "The place smells horrible when you come in from the street—cheese and furnace gas and clothes——"

"We haven't had her for two weeks," Norah explained.

"Well, I think that's hellish," Eve exclaimed under her breath.

"Evelyn," their mother said gently, distressed.

"Listen to my news," said Norah. "There's a man named Dunsmuir—Barry Dunsmuir, who offered me a job today."

"How'd you meet him, dear?"

"An ad—an ad in the paper. I answered it."

"Stenography?"

"That, and everything. It's quite complicated, I'll tell you about it. He's a scientist, a research man——"

"Don't trust him as far as you can see him," said Eve darkly.

Norah turned on her indignantly.

"What do you know about scientists, Eve Oliver?"

"Nothing," said Eve smoothly, "but he sounds to me like a crook!"

"He's very nice; he's quite old, in the thirties," Norah said mildly.

"Well, go on," Keith urged. "Is there money in it?"

"Yes, there is. But it isn't that——"

"Ah, no!" Keith interpolated in the pause. "It never is that! Money? Not with the Olivers. Oh, I know, we've got our faults, we're hot-headed, and we've devilish tempers! But we can't lie, and——"

"And we're never let off anything!" Norah finished it. It was a familiar chant; she and Keith always concluded it with what Eve sometimes witheringly characterized as their "idiot laughing at nothing."

"Well, go on, when you've settled the moral status of the Olivers," their mother said patiently when they stopped, and this started them off again.

"No, but, Norah," Keith asked, suddenly businesslike, "have you got a job really?"

"I have, and a first month's salary in advance.

I paid twenty-one dollars to the grocer and twelve to the butcher, and I bought you all modest Christmas offerings."

"You didn't!"

"I say I did. And a turkey too. He's on his way here."

"Alone?" Keith asked. "A young turkey in this great city?"

And so light were their hearts at the first sign of a break in the wall of their troubles and responsibilities that he and Norah could burst into laughter again.

"The moment you see him," Norah said, "you'll see that he's a turkey in whom you can have implicit confidence. Not handsome, no. Your first impression may be that he is almost *too* pure—too cold and quiet and reserved. Life has picked him, stripped him, you see that——"

"Oh, Norah, shut up!" Eve said impatiently, "and tell us about your job!"

"There's only one odd thing about it," Norah said, sobering. "Mr. Dunsmuir has a place in some little New Jersey town—village, rather. There's a school camp there, and some summer schools, and I guess that's about all. Foxaway Farm—isn't that a cute name? We'd have to live there."

"I tell you it sounds to me like a murderer!" Eve said.

"Once and for all, Nono, I couldn't let you go away with a man we don't know to a place like that," Mrs. Oliver said.

"He'd want you too, Mother. I—I insisted on that."

"Dearest child! But where is it?"

"Well, you go to Chester Junction, and then to—to Lake Cattahunk, I think he said, and there's an old servant in the place who'll have it warm and comfortable—nobody's lived in it for years."

"Honestly, Norah, you'll never get out alive!" This was Eve again.

"It's perfectly simple, Mother, and it would mean no rent for us, and that Keith could go off to Guatemala."

"What's he want to pay you, Norah?"

"About—I guess about a hundred a month."

"I'd do a lot of guessing about a thing like that," Eve said scathingly. "He'd probably offer you anything because he doesn't intend to pay it."

"A married man, dear?"

"No, he's not been married."

"And a scientist?"

"There was a scientist in a movie," Eve contributed. "Boris Karloff, I think it was, and his entire cellar was a series of cells—regular jail cells, for his human experiments. Of course, I know that was bunk," she said proudly as they laughed, "but I must *say* that I think Norah's simply crazy if she rushes off to New Jersey on any such wild proposition as that!"

"He's writing a book," Norah persisted patiently. "He has all the data and the specimens and the notes, and he wants to get it done. He's an explorer and he associates—he's been on trips with—with Sassoon."

"Is that right?" Keith said, suddenly interested, in the pause.

"Yes, and he's going off with Professor Sassoon right away," Norah went on, warming under a little encouragement. "There's an expedition to the South Pole——"

"Sure. I read you and Mother a lot about that a while ago," Keith said.

"I don't remember. Anyway, Mr. Dunsmuir wants to go very soon—in a few days, in fact, on the escort ship as far as Hobart, and he'd want Mother and me—and he said Eve too, or anyone we wanted—to go up and get the New Jersey place running and get some sort of servant in, and be all ready when he comes back to let him get to work. When Dr. Sassoon goes on to—South Georgia, or somewhere, then he'll come back."

"Why isn't he going all the way?" Eve asked suspiciously.

"He hasn't very good eyes, he wears strong glasses."

"A disguise!" Eve exclaimed.

Norah laughed.

"Well, it's a job," she observed simply.

"Yes, I know. But what a job!"

"I wish," Norah said, looking from Keith to Mrs. Oliver, "I wish you two would decide it for me. Mr. Dunsmuir is a gentleman; he's a Princeton graduate, and he did extra work at Oxford. He's all alone—no family. He would come out here and talk to Mother if she would like him to, Friday—they sail Saturday. It would mean that we lived 'way out in the country, but we'd have no rent and no living expenses, and I could save all my money. Keith wants to get out anyway, and Eve——"

"Exactly. What about me?" said Eve. "I could give swimming lessons in Lake Cattahunk all through January and February. When your body was discovered after the ice was cut, Crippen and I could——"

"Oh, Eve, shut up!" Norah exclaimed, in a rare burst of temper and nerves. "It's serious. The situation here is—desperate, isn't it, Keith? We've looked for jobs everywhere, we've tried everything. You're making sixteen a week, and that's absolutely all——"

"Excuse me," Eve, somewhat subdued, interposed politely, "I'm making nothing. They laid off seventeen of us this morning to take effect after New Year's."

"Well!" Norah said, and sat back. Suddenly she looked very tired.

"A hundred a month and a place to live, and Mother there too," Keith said. "I think you'd be crazy to turn it down!"

"He has references, dear? There's some way in which we can know that he isn't an impostor?"

"He has an office: Coates & Goldman, they're engineers. I was there once. And there was a judge, old Judge Bailey, who called him 'Barry,' and told me he had been best man when Mr. Dunsmuir's father and mother were married."

"Judge James Bailey?" This was Keith.

"I don't know."

"I could telephone him easy enough tonight, Mother."

"Is he in love with you, Nono?" Eve demanded suspiciously.

"Who? The old Judge? No, I hardly think so. He only saw me——"

"I mean this Dinwoodie murderer."

"Mr. Dunsmuir?"

"I don't think that's a very nice question to ask your sister, dear," Mrs. Oliver said with dignity.

"After all," Norah, who had her own reasons for remaining amiable, offered mildly, "it's any port in a storm now, isn't it?"

"Yes, why the deuce are we so picky and choosy?" Keith demanded roundly. "It's a home, and it's a living, and the minute Mother or Norah doesn't like it, she can get out. Girls have given up jobs before this. My worry would be," Keith added rationally, "as to whether Nono can handle it. It sounds like a sort of working-housekeeper job, on top of the stenography——"

"Darling boy, if one of the old family servants is there, I can do a lot of that!" Mrs. Oliver interrupted him eagerly.

Norah listened as one in a dream. They were so sure they were capable of deciding all about it, and they did not know anything at all! Why, she was actually to marry this man from whom they were afraid to accept even the most casual employment. Or was it a dream that he wanted her to marry him right away, day after tomorrow? They would feel rather flat if she told them the whole story and added that, upon serious reflection, she had decided to let Barry Dunsmuir go out of her life as completely and suddenly as he had entered it.

She was conscious of a weary, puzzled, philosophical sensation of letting the current carry her along; tomorrow would be Christmas, the family could talk all it liked until the day after Christmas, anyway. And there would be a turkey, and she, Norah, would still have money in her purse.

On Thursday she could decide. She was of

age; she could marry anyone she wanted to marry.

But, just the same, Norah could not sleep that night for thinking about it all. She wished she might confide in her mother; she did not dare. Her mother would forbid any such step definitely. She had taken Elinor's marriage to heart; she would perhaps collapse if Norah too suddenly announced similar plans. To marry a man she hardly knew, a man to whom she had spoken only a dozen times—under the circumstances this announcement might well kill her mother!

No, the only thing to do was to move to New Jersey, get established in the farmhouse at Foxaway, and then break the news gradually. Norah perhaps could suggest that she had known Barry "ever so long." Mother and Eve would know she hadn't, though, for she always told them everything she did and all about everyone she met. The family indeed complained that Norah had to be forcibly prevented from retailing the details of every chance encounter, every movie, every dream that formed part of her life. That was one reason all this secrecy was so strange and hard for her.

"If only Keith would really get started for his old Guatemala," she thought, "and if Eve would stay with Elinor for a while! Not that Elinor has much room in that little place. . . .

"If I were just alone with Mother I could explain. But they'd *fuss* so!

"Perhaps," she thought, tired out at last, and dropping off to sleep just as the church bells rang for midnight, "perhaps he'll wait until he gets back from Hobart to get married. Then, if he came up to the farm, and he and I didn't like each other . . .

"He's so smart, and he's generous too. I wish I liked him a little better, or loved him, or something!"

Chapter VIII

ON THE day after Christmas, a dark, forbidding day, with a feeling of snow in the air, Norah met Barry for luncheon at the old Brevoort Hotel restaurant, far down Fifth Avenue, and they discussed a meal that he assured her was very like Paris.

"In the food?" Norah asked, nervously making talk.

"That, yes. The bread and the onion soup and that big bowl of cold prunes. And the atmosphere too. You'd like Paris. I hate it."

"What makes you think I'd like what you hate?"

"Because all the ladies go wild over Paris."

"Do you—rather despise women?" the girl asked simply.

The elfin face opposite her wrinkled with his silent laughter.

"I estimate them about where they belong, Norah."

"Where you think they belong!" she corrected it, nettled.

"Where I think they belong."

"As inferiors."

"Well," he smiled, shrugging. "You see, I

never happen to have read the great books women have written," he explained, "I mean books that compare to Shakespeare and Milton and Dante and Goethe. I don't happen to know the work of the modern woman novelist who is as good as Tolstoi or Ibsen or Henry James. Just don't happen to!—The chicken is for the lady, and I'm having the eggs," Barry interrupted himself to say in rapid French. "No," he went on, enjoying himself, "the great plays, the great pictures that women have done have escaped me somehow. I don't remember enjoying any opera, by a woman, as much as I enjoy Wagner or Puccini. The classic symphonies—Bach and Tschaikowsky and Brahms—they satisfy me, and I never go on to those even finer compositions that women have given the world. There must be such, Norah—feminine classics, I mean. It would hardly be that one sex had given the world all its music and art, all its literature and science, all its explorers and medicine men. That couldn't be, could it?"

Norah was ready for him.

"Perhaps," she said serenely, "those things are not so important as you think."

"You interest me!" He was in the teasing, triumphant mood she hated. "What is more important, then?"

Norah looked at him steadily, with sapphire gray eyes.

"I should hate to think that—anyone I liked," she said, "would never find out!"

The man was silent, watching her, and she saw the expression of his face change. It changed to the look she liked: wistful, puzzled, lonely. He said simply:

"You're a funny little wench, Norah. But—but what you think has—has weight with me."

Disarmed for the moment, she watched him in silence as he paid his bill, and they went out together into the heavy winter shadow of the Avenue. Barry hailed a cruising taxicab and said, "City Hall, please!" and Norah, like a woman in a dream, got in.

"We are going to get a marriage license; we are going to be married!" she thought vaguely. It was all unreal. The City Hall seemed like some place she had seen before; a sense of having done all this before confused her as she followed Barry to the marriage license bureau.

Their business was quickly settled; it was when they were outside and coming down the steps again that Norah said suddenly:

"I'm sorry—just a minute. I—I don't want to be married."

The whole big grim winter city seemed to hum and throb and grind its great wheels in the silence. Barry, a step ahead of her, turned back with a sharp frown.

"What's the matter?"

Cold tears filled her eyes.

"I just don't want to."

"I thought we had it all settled."

"We did. But—but now I can't."

She stood wretched, undecided, on the City Hall steps.

"What's happened?"

"It's just," she argued feebly, evasively, "that I think we ought to—that I don't see why we don't wait until you get back."

"That's an entirely different arrangement," Barry said, displeased. "In any case, it's only a matter of six or seven weeks. I happen to want to get married this way today. I like the idea. It appeals to me as sensible. You want something from me, I want something from you; we've settled the whole thing."

"But I don't think," she faltered miserably, "that we *ought* to be sensible about getting married."

"Ought?" He took her up sharply. "Who is to say whether we 'ought' to do a thing or not? Is someone else deciding that for us?"

"I'm deciding it for us!" she said suddenly, in a stubborn tone. "I won't do it; I can't. It isn't that I don't appreciate your—your wanting me, and answering that advertisement and the money and everything———"

"Cut that!" he said gruffly, not unkindly, and Norah's perplexed heart warmed suddenly to him again, and she wondered why, having gone so far, she was creating this scene now, on a cold, stern flight of municipal steps, with a stern winter sky overhead, and a wind like a wall of steel driving steadily against her legs.

"You don't like me?" Barry asked suddenly.

"Well——" Her hesitant syllable was answer enough. She hastened to qualify it. "But there are times when I—I love you!" she said eagerly, slowly following him down the steps.

He had her arm, he was racing her along the great business streets, and she heard him laugh.

"You don't like me, but you love me, is that it?"

"Well, not exactly."

They battled along for a while in silence, heads down to the wind.

"Here's your church," he said presently. "And now's your time to decide. Either we go through with this adventure or we don't! Day after tomorrow I leave the country. I get back early in March; I open the farmhouse anyway. It's for you to decide whether you meant what you said when you started this whole thing.

"I'm ready to go through with it. I like the idea. I think it's a darned sensible way to marry. And I think you're the sort of woman who could make a success of anything. Take it as a business, if you like, with so much bad and so much good —work it out!"

"That's just what I don't want to do," she all but wailed, "it *isn't* a business!"

Barry drew her into the shelter of the great church doorway, bent his strong glasses toward his raised wrist.

"It's twenty past three. How long do you want?"

"Give me—give me five minutes!" said Norah.

But in less than the stipulated five minutes she had made up her mind. She put both her gloved hands for a second on Barry's arm; looked up with distressed, apologetic eyes into his face.

"I'm so sorry! I thought I could, but I can't!" she stammered. And in another second she was running away from him, turning a corner, lost in the afternoon crowd of downtown New York.

Chapter IX

EARLY that evening a boy came to the Oliver apartment with a note. Norah, deep in dinner dishes, wiped her hands and read it so nervously, so confusedly, and with so fast-beating a heart that she could hardly see the words.

"Dear Miss Oliver," Barry had written, *"in case you wish to reconsider your rejection of my original proposal, please telephone me at my office or at the club."*

"What is it?" Eve, setting her wet dark bob with the aid of combs and towels and a propped mirror at the kitchen table, asked curiously.

"It's from Mr. Dunsmuir."

"Well, I think you're a fool!" Eve commented lazily.

"For turning it down?"

"Why, certainly! What," Eve demanded patiently pinning a wet lock tightly against a comb, "what do you *want?* Good heavens, most jobs are absolutely in the beaten track! This one, if he *was* a murderer, at least took you out of the groove! I'd have jumped at it."

"But you said—*you*——" Norah was beginning indignantly, when her mother's voice came from the bedroom.

"What was it, darling?"

"It's from Mr. Dunsmuir, just saying that if I want to change my mind to telephone him," Norah said mildly, going into the bedroom.

"I think you were pretty darned swift in turning it down!" Keith observed good-naturedly from his seat beside his mother.

"Yes, because, after all, what else have we?" Eve demanded pathetically.

"I thought you all were against it," Norah reproached them.

"Against it, darling! No. It was only that we want to be sure it isn't a trap."

"A trap!" the girl echoed scornfully. "Do you suppose Dr. Sassoon would take a man along, a scientist, if he was a murderer or a trapper——"

They all began to laugh. But in Norah's heart there was a little sting of regret. She had had a chance to marry this same friend of the great Sassoon, a Princeton man, an Oxford man, and a man who had said, in his contrary, impish way, that he liked her too, and like any other stupid, unimaginative office drudge she had been afraid to try her fate. Why, she might have her school or her restaurant or her nursing home, or any one of her many enterprises, in that same Foxaway farmhouse, and she had let it all go! A ridiculous, inconsistent fear that she was too late for it now stirred deep in her being.

"You may as well all know," Keith said, in the silence after the unexpected laugh, "that I'm sailing on the fifth. Mother knows, and she approves, don't you, Mom?"

"I think you know best, Keith. I know these are hard times," Mrs. Oliver said gently, bravely.

"But what on earth are *we* to do?" Eve demanded.

"Well, I thought Norah had this job."

"I think you're all as mean as you can be about it!" Norah said angrily. "At first you were all calling him a murderer and saying how awful it would be to move into the country now, and now you all act as if I'd thrown down the Vice-President of the United States! I saw Mr. Dunsmuir today, and I told him I didn't think we could do it——"

"Well, I think you're simply crazy!" Eve, studying the effect of her hairdressing in a mirror, said airily.

"The point is, dear, what *else* can we do?" Mrs. Oliver asked. Norah was beyond speech.

"Look," Keith said suddenly, "you can easily live on a hundred a month until he gets back, anyway. And then, if you don't like it—why, get out! We'll give this place up on the first, store most of the stuff, and you and Mother and Eve go up to Cattahunk. Try it—try it for six months anyway; what harm can it do? And by the way," he added, "I went down to Judge Bailey's court today and saw him, and asked him if he knew Mr. Barry Dunsmuir, and he said yes, like a son. Couldn't say enough about him! Said that old Dr. Dunsmuir, his uncle who left him a pot of money, was Judge Bailey's closest friend."

"You fool!" Norah said in her heart. "You always thought you'd like adventure; you'd take a chance! You poor fool."

"I'll call him in the morning," she said aloud.

"Call him now!" Eve advised her nervously. "He may have gotten someone else by morning. He hasn't got much time."

"I'll call him in the morning," Norah repeated with dignity. She turned back to her dish-washing.

When she did call the office number in the morning with Keith's and her mother's expectant eyes upon her, Mr. Dunsmuir was reported out. Norah left her number to be called, but the telephone did not ring—did not ring, and at twelve o'clock she went to market with a strange heavy feeling in her soul. Was she to haunt downtown offices for a few humiliating weeks, and find another job, and sink right back into the machine again? Were these streets and these humble markets and the shadow and thunder of the elevated road to be her world for all the years of her youth?

It was with a returning rush of blood to her heart that upon coming back to the flat she heard, less than an hour later, even through the closed door, the cackling laugh, the high imperious voice that could belong to no one in the world but Barry Dunsmuir. Nervousness and uncertainty returned too; the sensation with which she entered her own home was not all pleasant. But at least—at least she was to have another chance!

He was talking very happily with her mother and brother. Mrs. Oliver wore her big dressing gown and had the Christmas blanket about her knees; Keith had moved the red-eyed electric disk into the front room.

Barry was telling them all about the political situation in Guatemala: he had never been there, of course, but then, she thought with dim, ironic resignation, that wouldn't daunt Barry. He would still know more about it than anyone else in the world ever knew!

"Now, this is the proposition," he was presently saying, "I go off tomorrow for six or seven weeks. You pack up and move to Foxaway. It's a comfortable old place—probably in rotten repair now, but that can be fixed. I've already written the old caretaker, Huldah Barnard, that she's to get everything ready for you. I told her you'd be up the seventh or eighth—somewhere in there.

"I'll wire you when I get back, and come up at once. I'm anxious to get to work. Sassoon has given me a wonderful opportunity, but I'm not at all sure I ought to go with him, even as far as Tasmania. However," his gnomelike eyes sparkled behind the strong lenses, "however, I'll see the *Ladysmith*—that's the ship they've been fitting up in England. Nansen designed her, but she's practically been made over. She's got a shoe——"

He was off upon such fascinating topics as water-sponsons, sastrugi, ice pressure, and leads. Norah watched him, fascinated, afraid; she knew he was watching her, although he never glanced at her. At the end he turned to her smilingly, and abandoning his previous subject completely, said briskly:

"Well, now, the only thing is to ascertain whether Miss Oliver here has made up her mind or not?"

"I'll say she's made it up!" Keith said with a laugh.

"Mr. Dunsmuir," Mrs. Oliver said tremulously, "indeed, we feel we are all very fortunate in the arrangement."

"It'll be awfully cold and wintry up there for a while!" he reminded her quickly, warningly.

"Oh, I'm country bred," Norah's mother said, unafraid. "The first twenty years of my life were spent in a little Connecticut town. And we lived in Princeton, Mr. Oliver and I, when these children were little."

"Foxaway—I haven't seen it for years—but it isn't like Princeton. You think you want to go in for this, Miss Oliver?" Barry asked Norah.

She was a little pale.

"I'm sure I can make a—a go of it," she said with a little effort.

"Good! Then suppose," the man suggested in a businesslike fashion, "we step around to the bank. Traveling expenses, that sort of thing."

"Want me to get into some clothes and go round with you?" Keith, whose impromptu costume indicated that he had been taking a bath when the caller arrived, asked alertly.

"No, no, thanks!" What a saturnine calm this man had, Norah thought. His heart must be beating as fast as her own was, but his voice was as casually pleasant as ever. "No, your sister and I will fix it up!" he said. He watched her while she kissed her mother good-bye; turned back for another kiss.

"Now, Norah," he said, in the street. "Where shall it be? What's the nearest church?"

"I'd rather not have it right here where everyone knows me."

"Well—taxi, then!" They got into a taxi, and Barry said, "Nice people, yours. Nice boy, that brother. He'll get on."

Norah's frightened heart steadied a little, but she could not speak.

"Scared?" Barry asked, with an undisturbed sidewise glance.

"Not—not that, exactly."

"Nothing to be scared about," he said. "You know, Norah, if it weren't Sassoon—he's like a god to me! I've had the most wonderful experiences of my life with old Fred—I say if it weren't for Sassoon I don't think I could go away today."

Her face was scarlet; she made no answer. He could laugh at her even now.

"I'm going to like being married to you!" he said.

Of course he had the ring; the license. There would never be a technical hitch where Barry Dunsmuir was concerned, Norah thought, as they stood up to agree to the promises that would make them man and wife.

He did not kiss her, but then that wasn't in the bond. He took her at once back to her own neighborhood and her own bank. The little account was made in the name of Norah Oliver.

"You use your own judgment about telling your family everything," he said. "Well, how do you feel, Mrs. Dunsmuir?"

She met this sedately, but her cheeks were red with something like anger.

"I tried the name, writing it. Norah Dunsmuir."

"How'd it look?" he asked with relish.

"All right," she answered lifelessly.

"No, Norah," Barry said, as they walked toward her home doorway, "the ladies don't want to paint pictures and write operas. Those things aren't important to them, God bless them! No, they want a man, first and foremost; they'll work through him, or on him, I'll grant you that. But the man comes first; he's got to stand between them and the world in the last analysis. George Eliot, Sarah Bernhardt, Mary, Queen of Scots—anyone you like: they all collapse when the man makes his demands. It's a theory of mine, and, by George, it seems to me modern social conditions uphold it! There are thousands of women—divorced, unmarried, widowed, trying to make a go of life—without a man! It can't be done. Mate 'em, and give them a home and children to worry about, and they may amount to something. But until they've got the man question settled—— What's this?"

"This is our house," Norah said coldly. Her face was a mask. She had stopped short.

"So it is!" he said. "I wasn't noticing. Well, I have to get downtown and buy a thousand things. And I've got a new will to sign—that's part of going off with Sassoon always.

"If you and I prove," he said amiably, detaining her on her own entrance steps, "if we prove that marriage can be made rationally like other contracts, we'll have done something! What a play—eh? I might try that, when I get this book off my mind."

Norah, red-cheeked, looked at him. She said nothing.

"Well, good-bye, Norah. I'll cable you when we arrive and when I'm starting home."

"Good-bye," she said. Her tone was steel.

"You'll be getting up into New Jersey about the seventh?"

"About then."

"Huldah expects you. Good-bye!"

"Good-bye!"

She extended her hand, and he shook it. Then he turned, a slim, brisk, nervous figure, in his fur-collared coat, and was gone. Norah went slowly upstairs.

This was December twenty-seventh, two days after Christmas.

Chapter X

TEN days later the apartment in the Bronx was completely dismantled, and the Olivers were ready to go on their way to Foxaway Farm. Keith would not go with them: he had left the day before for Guatemala, and Norah and Eve and Anne Winter, his fiancée, and sister Elinor and her husband had all gone down to the dock to see him off.

Afterward the Olivers had had dinner at Elinor's house: the first time Mother had deigned to go there and recognize the status of the married runaways at all. "So there's *that* much gained by the break-up!" Norah thought.

She herself was beginning to get thoroughly depressed by this whole adventure. It seemed a tremendously daring thing, especially with Keith gone; Eve suspicious and skeptical; and Mother still weak and ill. And she herself was so tired!

Elinor's new husband, a bluff, boastful sort of person whom nobody liked much, had teased her about it.

"Why, you must be crazy, Norah," Bill Gunther had said. "What d'you want to go 'way up into the country this time of year for?"

Elinor, daintily serving cream of tomato soup, chicken, spinach, and hot biscuits, and a real magazine salad of endive and persimmons and cream cheese, and being very married, dutiful, sweet, and successful, had added her doubtful note.

"But, darling, do we have to go to such extremes? Dragging poor sweetheart Mother up there into God knows what inconvenience and cold! Couldn't you find jobs nearer home? It all sounds so—I mean so deliciously fantastic," Elinor had said.

"I shouldn't wonder if it was gangsters," Eve had suggested pleasantly, fluffing her hair at the mirror.

"You're all a lot of pals," Norah had said, "just good old staunch pals, seeing me through. Do you think *I* want to go up into northern New Jersey in January? What in the name of heaven was I to do——"

"We've got her mad!" Bill had said admiringly, as she paused.

"Yes, you have got me mad! Here we were, without any money——"

Norah had checked herself suddenly and had fallen silent. Why waste energy fighting with a great conceited sap like Bill Gunther? He was the only son of a rich mother who gave him all the money he needed. His opinion on her venture was utterly worthless.

She and Eve had taken their mother home rather early. Bidding good-bye to Keith, who had been a part of her life ever since she could remember anything at all, had been hard; parting with Elinor was suddenly tragic too.

"Come down to me if you hate it, Mother darling!" Elinor had said suddenly at the end, and Norah had been tired, cross, sad, and dirty enough to say sharply, "Oh, don't be a fool, Elinor! New Jersey isn't Siberia!"

"Precious child, I didn't mean that!" Elinor had said, in her new angelic, wifely, amused manner. "I only felt—and Billikins here feels too, that it's rather a wild venture, and that you may have enough of it very soon!"

"This city's the place to work," Bill himself had added, a big arm about Elinor's slimness and fineness, a good-natured grin on his broad face.

Norah offered no argument. She escorted her mother and sister in a taxi back to the forlorn five-room apartment that had been their home for more than two years.

The narrow, crowded rooms had never been attractive; they were completely desolate now. Floors were bare; packing cases stood open to receive the last of the spoons and hand towels; curtains were down, and the beds were stripped to mere sheets and blankets. Every little gallant device that had veiled, or tried to veil, the poverty and ugliness of the place was gone now; strange smells were abroad, the smells of spilled cinnamon, of dust, of ammonia, and of plumbing.

Norah was exhausted. Her hands were stiff and sore from packing; her mind was weary from excitement and emotion. To have in her heart the secret knowledge of her relationship with Barry Dunsmuir was agitating enough, without all the other burdens the day had developed. It had been an endless day.

All through it there had been the pain of the imminent parting with Keith—Keith, who had always been her buckler and her shield against anxiety and strain. Mother had cried all the last morning; Keith had not seemed to care as much about Mother as he did about what quiet, self-satisfied Anne was murmuring to him when she took him off for lunch.

Packers, plumbers, and van men had claimed Norah all morning; she had telephoned the big station to find out when trains went to Lake Cattahunk. There was a train at 2:40, it appeared, that reached Chester Junction at 4:42. From there there was a local at 5:10 for Mt. Pleasant, Woodport, and Cattahunk.

The late afternoon had been exciting, but tiring too. There had been little neighborhood accounts to settle; it was good to have the money with which to settle them. There had been a bursting suitcase to take to the Salvage Shop, and a load to deliver to the Salvation Army man. Empty milk bottles to the dairy; books back to the library; Eve and Norah had had to move fast to get home in time to dress and go down with Mother and Keith to the boat. And there Elinor and her Bill had joined them, and that had been a strain too. For there was no use pretending that Mother liked Bill or approved of him, or of the way he and Elinor had managed their affair.

Elinor had had to pretend to be perfectly at ease and very merry, and Bill had been more boisterous and self-satisfied even than was natural to him. But Mother had retreated into an icy magnificence as unnatural to her as their poses were to them. She had been polite, laboriously sympathetic and interested in their affairs, and Eve irritated and haughty, as she always was when things went wrong. The effect of their combined attitudes had been to make Norah frantic with nervousness, nor was her sisterly pride and devotion helped much by the constant complacent presence of Anne, whose daring, "Shall I come down on the next boat, Keith?" had apparently been the only part of the farewells heard by Keith at all. She came back to the flat tired, resentful, discouraged, to find Uncle Rodney there, as usual in hope of dinner and a loan.

"Somehow I feel," her mother said sadly the next day when they were doing the last things of all just before surrendering the keys to the apartment forever, "somehow I feel as if we might never have a real home again!"

"Mother, don't talk like that!"

"Well, I know, dear. But I'm not as young as I once was, and I'm not as strong. And somehow, to see so many of the dear old things going into storage, to have Elinor living on the other side of the city with that—that Gunther!—to have Keith gone, my only son, into one of those semi-civilized places, and to be taking just our suitcases like Arabs into a place we never saw before——"

"You make it sound like Tibet, Mother! It's New Jersey."

"I know, dear, but I can only express my feelings."

"I wish I could express mine without being arrested!" Norah thought. But outwardly she was calm—she had to be calm. Somebody had to be, and with Mother in this martyr mood, and Eve superior and silent, sniffing suspiciously as it were at every fresh stop, it was obviously for Norah to carry the load.

Being young, she presently discovered to her own surprise that she enjoyed her own share of it. She liked the sense of emergency and change, the feeling of saying good-bye to conditions and places that had been hard and unfriendly, liked buying tickets, hiring taxis, arranging for suitcases, porters.

When they were at last on their way she settled herself in the train with enormous satisfaction. After the furious exertions of the last few days it was restful to think that now for two long hours she could do nothing. She might look out of the windows peacefully, reveling in the sights that fled so smoothly by her; the last string had been tied, the last box labeled and dispatched to storage, the keys had been given to Olsen, with the old ice box and the broken box couch and the hall rug.

"What time do we get to Carter Junction, dear?"

"Chester Junction, Mother. At twenty minutes of five."

"It'll be pitch dark," Eve contributed.

Norah paid no attention. She was dreaming of the names. Chester Junction and Hopatcong and Cattahunk. And above all, Foxaway Farm. Would she come to know all these names and rattle them off smoothly——

The long tunnel, the blocks of masonry and steel that were apartment houses slid away; they had crossed under the river and were in more open country, bleak, ugly winter country today, with stripped trees and gardens willing to betray every shabby building, every garbage barrel and raw garage. But to Norah's eyes it was all fascinating and thrilling.

"Poor Daddy!" Mrs. Oliver said when they passed a big graveyard. Her eyes filled with tears. Norah glanced at her; said nothing. After all, Dad had been cremated, and his ashes were down in Princeton. However, if that was Mother's mood today——

"I hope this old housekeeper will realize that we are going to want baths and beds and hot supper!" the older woman presently said.

"Oh, she will! You know how fat and white country beds are," Norah observed hearteningly.

"I don't know how *you* do!" Eve said pointedly from her window.

"Well, Mr. Dunsmuir told me that he used to take friends up there from Princeton for house parties. There are seventeen rooms in the place. That sounds like lots of blankets and fireplaces."

"Well, let's hope!" Eve suggested dubiously.

"It would be dreadful, Norah, if he hadn't sailed after all, and had a house party up there now. I am disgracefully dirty," said her mother alarmedly, "and I really do not feel—I do *not* feel up to the slightest effort."

"Mother dear, he radioed me from the ship to say that his address was *'Ladysmith,* Hobart.'"

"Oh, yes," Mrs. Oliver said reassured. "I forgot."

"If there are any guests in the house," Eve said, "I am going to make it clearly understood——"

Her determined voice died away into a tone of brooding reflection. Just what she would make understood Eve had obviously not yet decided, but that it would be adequate when it came Norah had no doubt. She returned to her contemplation of the flying landscape and the wintry little towns and the river, with the smoky cold blur that was New York on the other side.

The countryside grew lonelier, looked colder. A sparse flutter of snow smeared the hot car windows. It was time to gather their belongings together, to stir themselves stiffly and drowsily. Next stop Chester Junction.

Dusk was thick upon the little railway town when they descended to the sooty platform. The other train, one car, with its engine steaming, was already waiting. The car was hot; a round-bodied coal stove had raised it and its red plush chairs almost to the suffocation point.

"We'll only be in it about twenty minutes, Mother."

"It doesn't start for twenty-eight!" Eve said.

They waited. There was only gray wintry dusk outside the windows now, and long before they started the mountain darkness was on the world. It really was frightening, Norah admitted in her soul, to be going so far away from home, into such a lonely place. She was glad they were all together, and had a spasmodic moment of aching longing for Keith. A man—any man, would have been a comfort, even Mr. Dunsmuir.

Norah, remembering his complacent references to woman's dependence upon her man, stiffened her back. After all, this was twentieth-century America, not medieval Sicily.

"You can't see a thing!" she announced from the window. The black panes only gave her back Norah Oliver's round, eager face, and the shabby fur of her old coat collar, and the curve of her hat.

"Really, I'm not trying to make difficulties, but I *really* don't think we ought to go on with this!"

This was Eve. Norah looked at her patiently.

"Oh, why not, Eve?" Mrs. Oliver faltered.

"Well, Mother, if anything did happen, it might be days—*months,* before anyone took the trouble——" Eve was beginning with a great air of temperance and reason, when the brakeman opened the car door letting in an icy blast of cold mountain air.

"Cattahunk!" he shouted. Without further argument the Olivers got out.

The station was a mere box, with snowflakes fluttering timidly over it. All about the harshly lighted station platform there was complete bewildering darkness, and when the train had snorted away there was appalling silence as well.

"Good gracious, Nono?" Mrs. Oliver said questioningly.

Norah banged on a locked freight-room door against which dim old posters still announced summer dances and the renting of canoes. An old man came up behind her with a lantern, one mittened hand hooped about his ear. She shouted at him.

Sure he knew the Dunsmuir fa'm. Foxaway, that was it. Huldy Ba'nnard was there: "Thet's right, she doos live there!" the old man said brightly. He'd git the folks a car en git 'em up that way if they wunted he should.

"Is there a hotel?" Norah demanded.

"Yes'm, there's some reel big hotels up Mount Pleasant way and round Espanong. All summer long ye'll see——"

"But now. I mean *now*."

"No'm, there ain't no hotel here now," the old man said, a little dashed.

"But there must be someone who takes boarders?"

"Not now, there ain't. Mis' Muzzell she's gone to live with Joe for a spell, en the Youngers, they're both reel sick this winter. But don't Huldy expect ye? Seems to me my datter was sayin' Huldy expected the folks up some time in now."

"Well, she does expect us, of course," Norah said, reassured. "But it seems funny she didn't send in a car or something."

"I'll git ye out there!" the old man said alertly. "I'll git my datter's car."

He tottered swiftly away; the Olivers hardly spoke in his short absence. It was bitterly cold on the station platform, and the snow continued to fall uncertainly. They could see the gently twisting flakes in the raw light that gushed down from a single powerful globe, dangling over the station.

With their luggage, they silently squeezed themselves into the dilapidated car that presently chugged up to the freight scales, and were off into the unknown. A lean young man was driving the car; Norah, on the front seat with him, asked him sociably if the old man was his father. "My grandpap!" the boy answered briefly. He spoke only once again to say:

"Here we be! But what you folks come up here for this weather has me beat all hollow!"

The night was completely black; they had only the feeble car lights by which to see the bulk of an old farmhouse in the gloom. It showed no sign of light or life. Norah supported her mother with a strong young arm. Her heart was beating fast.

"Huldy!" shouted the driver. "Huldy Ba'nnard!"

Wind was crying softly about the place, and shutters creaked. For some minutes there was no other sound. But presently they heard a window rasp up. A voice came down, for the first few phrases unintelligible, but finally to be defined as elderly and female and agitated. It was angry, startled, apologetic by turns.

Presently a kitchen entry door opened a few feet away from them, showing a dim, cavernlike interior lighted apparently by one feeble lamp. A tall, vociferous woman was among them, addressing herself exclusively to the boy.

"Chess, if you tell your aunt Emma this on me, I'll never git over it!" said this individual loudly. "I ben reel ill—hed the doctor in a spell back, and I lay I forgot the folks was comin'. Hed two dispatches, too, from Alice Dunsmuir's boy. I declare I don't know when I've ever done a thing like this, if I did then! Your mother and your aunt Emma'll hev it on me 'tel the day I die! I ain't—— However," Huldy interrupted herself, noticing the huddled group of newcomers for the first time, "step in, folks, and we'll see what we kin do. We don't need you no longer, Chess, and thanks for gittin' 'em here! No need blue-mouldin' out here in the snow. Looks to me like a real hard storm, the way it's warmin' up. Come in."

The car chugged away into blackness; the Olivers entered a large dim kitchen smelling of ashes, apples, dish-water, smelling sharply of mice. It was weakly lighted by one kerosene lamp. The enormous range was cold; a pool of water stood forlornly on its expanse of rusted iron. The heaviness of the grave was in the room.

Mrs. Oliver sat limply down in a chair: she shuddered with a sudden chill. Eve turned her back upon Norah and Huldah and burst into tears. Norah saw facing her a large, raw-boned woman of perhaps seventy, with a scraggle of gray hair wound severely off in a knob at the back of her head, teeth missing from her wide smile, and a costume of colorless wrappers superimposed upon colorless wrappers to an extent that disguised her figure completely.

"I guess I look like Astor's pet gander all right!" said this apparition. "But I ben real lame lately, an' I haven't got about hardly none. I was goin' up to my sister's tomorrow, if it didn't snow too heavy, an' tell her some friends of Mr. Dunsmuir's was comin' up, an' we had to git ready for 'em. Looks like I've lost track of the days—dun't seem possible it's the seventh a'ready."

"Well, that's all right!" Norah said staunchly. "Only it's too bad to have gotten you out of bed. The thing is, we want supper, you see, and somewhere to sleep."

"I was goin' to git your blankets all aired for

ye, there!" Huldy lamented, clapping her hands together.

"What could we eat?" Norah said brightly, with chattering teeth. The cold of the kitchen seized upon her like gripping hands.

"Listen——" This was Eve, drying her eyes, blowing the cold tip of her pretty nose, facing Huldah with hostility. "We can't stay here! This is—ghastly. Where is the nearest hotel?"

Huldah looked at her curiously, even with faint admiration.

"You look for all the world like a cousin of mine, May Block," she said, pleased. "There's no hotel here, dear, an' I may as well tell you the truth."

"My mother is ill," Eve began fiercely. Huldy merely looked at her vaguely and turning to Norah said apologetically:

"I lay I don't believe there's one thing in this house you could eat for supper! Now, ain't it a shame we let Chess go?—he could've got Ken Lassen to open the grocery."

"Telephone!" Eve commanded angrily. Neither Huldah nor Norah paid any attention to her.

"There must be tea?" Norah asked patiently, sweetly.

"Oh, there's tea and flour and preserves!" Huldy answered. "But I ben feeling so poorly I jest ben heatin' myself milk on my karosene stove up to my room. My sister br'ut me over some soup an' a pie, Sunday. 'Huldy,' s'says——"

"Would it take long to get this stove going?"

"Well, there it is, dear. I had this dizzy spell a while back, and Doc said my leaning down over the stove an' gittin' my face s'hot——"

"But here's wood; here's coal!" Norah said desperately, opening the great door that led from the back of the kitchen to enormous pantries, woodsheds, outhouses. "We'll have to get this room warm on account of my mother. She's been ill. You tell me what to do and I'll do it."

She took off her coat, draped it over her mother's shoulders.

"It's really bed that I need, Nono. I feel so tired, dear."

"We'll have to have hot water for your bottle, anyway!" Norah crumpled paper in hands that were cramped with fatigue. Huldy struck matches.

"The rooms upstairs is awful cold," Huldy volunteered.

"Well, we'll get this warm, and get warm ourselves, and then see." Norah filled the heavy iron kettle at the sink pump. The wood fire crackled, and Huldah dumped upon it a scuttleful of coal calculated, Norah thought, to extinguish the Great Fire of London.

"When's the next train!" Eve exclaimed rather than asked.

"There's a train tomorrow at noon," Huldy answered, and Norah could almost have laughed at the laconic brevity of the words.

"There's milk back in the cold pantry," Huldy presently observed. "The Tebbitts leave me a pan every night. There must be three days' milk there——

"An' there's roots down cellar——"

"Roots! What do you think we are, guinea pigs?" Eve burst forth. Norah came out of the pantry with a great tin of rough oats.

"We'll have oatmeal," she said, "and tea with cream. And there are plum preserves."

"You kin skim all the cream you want off them pans in the entry closet. They've jest been a-settin' there."

"Mother, you'll soon be enjoying a large bowl of oatmeal and cream, and that'll warm you up. But, Huldy," Norah said, "we'll have to sleep down here tonight. We'll have to bring the mattresses and blankets down and sleep here somehow."

Huldah, as the steadily increasing heat from the stove began to make the room habitable, had seated herself in a rocker and wrapped her arms about her. She rose alertly.

"Well, you're one to think things out: I see that the minute you come! I'll show ye where we can get some beddin'," she said admiringly.

Presently the oatmeal began to smack and bubble on the stove; the kettle whispered. Mrs. Oliver gingerly loosened her outer wraps; Norah, standing by the stove, felt that just as she never before had been so forlornly cold and hungry and wearied in her life as she had been tonight, so she had never found warmth and the prospect of food and rest so enchanting.

All about the kitchen blankets were draped, airing; pillows gave forth a faint sour smell in the heat. Three mattresses lay on the floor, on each fresh linen country sheets were crumpled, warming. Norah found soup plates, kitchen spoons, sugar. She skimmed from Jersey milk cream clotted and pale brown.

Above the old house the rising wind whined with increasing distress. The beams creaked within, and bare branches clicked an answer from the farmyard without. The cold, the dreary smells of mice and dish-water and old boards gave way to the heartening scent of tea, of oatmeal, of a bright coal fire. The warming linen was scented sweetly with lavender.

"Now, if it gits too warm for you folks in the night——" Huldah said.

"Oh, kill her, somebody!" Eve, her head on the table, her arms locked about it, moaned feebly.

WIFE FOR SALE

"She's a card!" Huldy commented on this approvingly.

Norah was beginning to dish the sweet, hot, firm oatmeal. The old clock in the kitchen of Foxaway Farm wheezed seven.

Chapter XI

THE cascading of coal on the fire awakened Norah; winter dawn was gray at the uncurtained, unshaded windows of the old kitchen. The bent figure of Huldy, spare and bony, and clothed in a belted chocolate percale, was at the stove. Norah stirred in her oddly assorted bedding, and Huldy, replacing the nest of iron rings that was the only stove opening, turned to smile at her grimly.

"Morning?" Norah whispered.

"Morning! It's 'most eight," Miss Barnard returned with relish. "I thought you folks was goin' to sleep the day out!"

"How do you feel?"

"I don't feel—" Huldy opened one of the smaller rings, looked into the range, "I don't feel none too good," she admitted.

Norah sat up, and every bone in her young body responded sorely to the fatigues of yesterday and the cramped discomfort of the night. Her fingers and her nose felt cold, and her face sleepy and warm.

The scene was not inspiring. Three mattresses littered a large part of the kitchen's free space;

each was a jumble of blankets and pillows, with the casually strewn contents of three separate suitcases to add further confusion. A silent hump in one of these nests, with a snarl of dark hair at the top of it, was Eve; she did not stir. The hump on the next floor bed moved, however, and Mrs. Oliver looked cautiously forth from a curve of blanket.

"Norah, is it morning?"

"Eight o'clock."

"My gracious!" Norah's mother raised herself; subsided again. "It's bitter cold!" she said. "I heard the wind all night."

"Did you sleep at all, Mother?"

"I don't think I slept very much," Mrs. Oliver said, sighing. "Well, Norah, this is an adventure, isn't it?"

"In a word, yes," Norah agreed, struggling out of bed. She groped about amid the covers for her own belongings: slippers, an old wrapper. Huldy, hugging her own shoulders, had drawn a rocking chair close to the stove.

"My sister's husband come by about five," volunteered Huldy, "an' I'm going back with him to Matty's."

"About *five!*"

"Yes, 'twas real dark. I got my candle lighted an' come down to the side door. Seems he run out of oil cake, an' he come down for a sack. Seems Matty's all upset about my feelin' so poor, an' she wants I sh'd come up to her for a spell. I's thinkin'," Huldy added, as Norah made no sign, "if you folks are stayin' for some time——?"

"We're going back to the city this morning," Eve said, from a looped Shaker bonnet of blanket.

"Go on," Norah said, putting the filled kettle on the stove.

"I's thinking that I could stop at the store for ye, if so be's there's anything you needed," Huldy finished.

"We ought to have some groceries—some bread, anyway," Norah said.

"I told Ollie to bring some bread."

"Coffee?" Mrs. Oliver suggested.

"There's coffee here."

"That was Chess Adams come round with you last night," Huldy further explained; "his mother's my cousin, and her husband's sister is Emma Taft. Emma's got a girl, Pauline, who'd come up here and help you some, any time you'd like it. She's an awful big, stout girl, and she's stronger'n most boys."

"I wish you'd send her 'round," Norah said. She gathered her own bed and bedding into a great roll, dropped them in a corner out of the main line of march.

"Norah," her mother said pleadingly, "we

mustn't talk as if we could stay here, dear. Really—*really*——!"

It was a long time before Norah answered her, except with a puzzled, half-smiling glance of sympathy.

Huldy's brother-in-law returned with bread and a round, flimsy bakery ring of coffee cake, and Norah paid for them. Huldy, with every kindly wish for the comfort of the three Olivers, departed, after a long demonstration of how the oil stove, brought down from her vaultlike chamber, worked, and incidentally how it smelled. The range dampers were also explained to the attentive Norah; the fire strengthened, the kitchen was hot.

Norah and Eve and their mother breakfasted informally on smoking coffee decorated with rich brown blobs of cream, rich stiff country jam, fresh scrambled eggs as delicate as fresh flowers, and the spongy cheap grocery bread.

After breakfast, dirty, warm, weary, well fed, the temptation was to fall into a dreamy stupor of idleness. But the arrival of Emma Taft's Pauline was invigorating. Pauline was an enormous, tall, energetic girl who was versed in the ways of country kitchens.

The morning raced away. At Pauline's suggestion a door was opened into an adjoining apartment known as the "kitchen chamber." The round-bellied iron stove in the place was fired, and when it was warm enough to be entered, Pauline and Norah and Eve carried the bedding in there. There were already two old beds in the place, with exhausted-looking rust-stained mattresses; Norah was amazed to see how the whole situation, mental, moral, physical, improved when the beds were decently made, the contents of the suitcases put into drawers, and the kitchen cleared of its overnight tenants.

Lunch had to be more eggs, more tea and spongy bread, more jam; but the invaluable Pauline had found various "roots" in the cellar, and the real luxury of the meal was supplied by a rich dark Hubbard squash. baked in broken squares, hot, filling, sweet.

"I'd 'a' made ye a pudding," Pauline said, "if I could 'a' laid my hands on Huldy's vanilly."

Norah loved this Pauline already. Work simply vanished beneath her ungainly, red-knuckled hands; her presence meant comfort.

"How do we get to the store, Pauline?"

"Well—we ain't got no car. Ef I could git hold of my brother Johnny——"

Pauline wiped the hot empty dish-pan with a rag, turned the pan upside down, hung the rag on the hot pipe that ran above the range.

"I could walk over to Mis' Abbot's," she finally said. "Her George'll take me down."

With money and a list she departed, and the

Olivers sat down to their luncheon and their talk.

"You do as you like, Norah," Eve said, "but I will *not* stay here!"

"You don't have to stay here," Norah assured her.

"I don't see," Mrs. Oliver began, brightly reasonable, "how any of us can stay here. In the first place, it's extremely—it's *amazingly* uncomfortable, and in the second place, I don't see that we accomplish anything. I don't blame Mr. Dunsmuir: he hasn't seen the place for years, and he probably remembers it as a boy would in the summer vacations.

"But this dreadful woman, Huldah, who was supposed to have everything in order, and warm, and food in the house——!"

"Food in the house is nothing. A bathroom in the house is what I am just silly enough to like!" Eve said.

"Well, Huldah was sick," Norah offered mildly.

"Her being sick or well wouldn't affect the plumbing," Eve suggested.

"It's as good as Washington had!"

"Yes, dear, and Cleopatra had no limousine! And they're both dead."

"Well, they didn't die as a result——"

"Oh, girls, girls," Mrs. Oliver said. "This is the way I see it," she went on, as both the girls laughed rather shamefacedly. "This is no time of year to come to the country. We must go back and make some temporary arrangement until Mr. Dunsmuir returns in March. *Then,* if he wants Norah to come up here, and it's warm and sunny, it will all be quite different. Doesn't that seem a more reasonable plan?"

"But where would we go, Mother?"

"Well, to some very modest little hotel, I suppose."

"I'll get a job," Eve announced. "I'll not come up here ever again. Not under chloroform!"

"We haven't money enough for that," Norah protested. "Mr. Dunsmuir has advanced four hundred dollars—one hundred at Christmas, and three hundred that he put in the bank for me. Of that, half is gone—we have only a little more than two hundred dollars left. How far would that go if we had to pay hotel rent and all our meals? It wouldn't last three weeks.

"Here, we could live three months on it, easily."

"But, Norah, what then, darling?"

"Why, then it will be summer, Mother, and warm and comfortable here, and Mr. Dunsmuir'll be home, writing his book, and I'll have a hundred-dollar job with all expenses paid.

"Darling, you really think we can *stand* this?"

"Well, if we don't, we merely owe Mr. Dunsmuir four hundred dollars, and we've broken up the city place for nothing."

"I don't think you ever should have borrowed it," Eve said firmly.

Norah said nothing. But there was a stubborn set to her jaw.

In mid-afternoon, when the kitchen was quiet and orderly, and some concoction of beef and vegetables was simmering under Pauline's careful eye on the stove, the three newcomers buttoned themselves into their heavy coats and went on an inspection of the new home.

A long dining room, with windows north and south, bisected the house. It had a great gaunt smoke-stained fireplace, a good table, forlorn chairs; it smelled coldly of long-ago meals. Beyond it was a square hall, with a fine old boxed stairway, and a glass-panelled front door with a dirty fanlight. Two large rooms flanked the hall: one almost empty, with a doctor's table and some medical books for its chief furnishing; the other, a big, charming country parlor, where there were a horse-hair and walnut set, a clock under a glass bell, a fireplace, some dim old portraits, hooked rugs, and a hanging lamp in chains. Many books—lines of them, dim and fascinating and full of promise, ranged in old bookcases along the walls. The window of this room, south and west, would look into the garden, when the garden came back from under the snow; they had no under curtains, but their many panes and fine lines were disguised under long dangling ropes of rotted and moth-eaten rep. An old square piano, covered in scalloped plum-colored flannel, completed the inventory of the room's furnishing.

Upstairs were bedrooms, one after another, all large and with many windows. But there was no bathroom, and the closets were mere shallow niches in the corners. Everywhere were deep fine window sills, fine old shutters, and heavy white-painted doors rounded at the top. And here and there, among the cheaper pieces, were good chairs, good chests, mirrors of fine and even elegant lines.

And everywhere were dirt, decay, neglect. The windows were filthy; curtaining and bedding were tumbled roughly together, books had fallen to the floor, rugs were awry, dead flies were piled on tables and sills, paper had moulded on the walls and fallen in long plastery streamers. Cold had the house in its bitter grip; the women shivered as they went gingerly about on the littered floors.

They went back to the kitchen, which seemed a haven of refuge after the bleakness and the gray winter shadows of the house.

"What do people do in a place like this?" Eve demanded, when they were sitting in their respective chairs about the stove. "It kills you to get up and get dressed, you're never clean, you have to slave to get warm, and get anything to eat, and fill lamps, and sweep. And then you go to bed again. Is that the way country people live, Mother?"

"I suppose they do, dear."

"There are a thousand things we could do here," said Norah.

"As what?"

"Oh, in a place like this? Run a hotel, or open a roadside restaurant, or have a school. Or you could put up jam or bake bread or have a summer camp for kids; there are a thousand things, aren't there, Mother?"

"I suppose so," Mrs. Oliver conceded rather dubiously, with a little preliminary clearing of her throat.

"Well, we'll be comfortable tonight," Eve said, "and I go down on the noon train tomorrow."

"What do you think, Norah?" the mother quavered.

"I'm thinking. I like it," Norah confessed suddenly.

"Oh, Norah, act your age! A Trappist monk couldn't live here!"

"It's—ours," Norah went on, as if she were thinking, rather uncertainly, aloud.

"It is not ours. It belongs to a man we hardly

know, who is cruising off in the South Seas somewhere——"

"I mean in this way it's ours," Norah elucidated, as her sister paused on an indignant note. "It's—got possibilities. It might be very thrilling to be the secretary of a man here. It would be different."

"You said it," Eve agreed inelegantly.

"I mean—I have to stick it," Norah finished.

"You don't!"

"I say I do."

"Oh, come, let's not be heroic; let's not be Casabiancas sitting in the hole in the dyke at this late date!" Eve exclaimed scornfully.

"Swimming the Hellespont, you mean," Norah suggested.

"I don't care what he did, I know he was one of those smug smarties who tell everyone else how to do everything!" Eve countered unabashed.

"Well, after all, I did enter upon a contract with Mr. Dunsmuir——" Norah began mildly.

"You didn't sign anything!"

"Only a marriage register," Norah thought. Aloud she said, "Well, I'm going to stay. And you can go down and live with Elinor if you like, and look for a job. Only, while you *are* here, Eve, do try to see it as a sort of adventure —as fun——"

"Fun!" Eve echoed. But this was a new note

from Norah, and Eve was a little impressed. Norah had gained in firmness, somehow.

Eve penetrated to the tomblike parlor again and returned with books. She gave her mother a bound copy of *Godey's Lady's Book,* and Mrs. Oliver, warm and fed and resting by the stove, turned its pages in amusement. Eve, waiting for the kettle to boil before beginning piecemeal ablutions in the bedroom off the kitchen, opened *Pride and Prejudice*.

"I've never read anything of Austen's. I suppose you ought to," Eve observed, in the most agreeable and mollified tone she had used for twenty-four hours.

Norah had bundled herself up again for more investigations and some fresh air. She left the two in the kitchen with a repetition of her former inexplicable phrase, "I tell you I like it. But I'm—thinking it out."

She went through a door back of the stove into a sort of laundry passage, where there were wooden tubs, ropes, ladders, stove wood and fire wood, coal, kerosene tins, all the litter of a kitchen annex, with empty jam glasses aligned on a cobwebbed windowsill, and a rickety stairway ascending to some sort of lair above.

Beyond was a long line of linked sheds; more wood, more ladders and farm machinery, and finally, off at an angle, a feed room, smelling sweetly of oats and clean sacking, and a slippery open walk powdered with snow, beyond which again were a chicken house and a chicken run, whose inhabitants appeared to feel mournful and resentful in the cold.

Then came the old-fashioned great stable and the hay barns, set in a strange jumble. Norah went from one to the other like a fascinated child, unfastening leather thongs at the doorways, loving every trough and whitewashed plank, every homely rustic makeshift in the way of mangers and stalls.

There were hens in the barn too, fluffing and snuggling in the hay. Norah frightened herself when she frightened one, and starting back, looked down at the improvised nest where the hen had been. Why—what was it——

She stopped, laughing. It was only an egg, warm and white, with a curled little warm feather clinging to it. Only an egg, but Norah had never found a fresh egg before. She went on, carrying it carefully, ridiculously thrilled by the adventure.

The ground was rising now, and outside the barns the bare limbs of enormous elms and maples were moving in the wind. At the upper end of the farmstead Norah let herself out through a great hay door and was suddenly in the barnyard.

The door slammed behind her; she braced her back against it to get her bearings before going farther, for the wind was fitful. An early January twilight was softening the outlines of the world; everything was very still, in a sort of late afternoon hush between the rushes of the wind, and the sun which had been hidden all day was smouldering low against a patch of stripped young alders toward the west and sending bloody angles and shafts across the sheds and fences.

Foxaway stood on rising ground with low mountains rolling away from it in three directions. Down the hill, in the direction Norah, with her back against the barn door, was facing, a road bordered by enormous trees ran a straight quarter of a mile to the village. On each side of the road were stone fences, fields, and occasional strips of dense heavy woodland; the hills behind the farm were thickly wooded and deep in snow.

The village was lifeless; the shabby clapboarded and scattered houses had drawn into themselves for the long cold season; smoke rose dreamily from their chimneys into the last red winter light; there was no other moving thing to be seen except when a mud-spattered motorcar moved for a few blocks, stopped again.

Over the whole world, the fields and roads, the hills and fences, and the great denuded trees, the winter night was deepening. The sky turned gray, masses of black cloud formed themselves on the western horizon. Here and there, in the village, a speck of yellow showed where a lamp had been lighted in some farmhouse kitchen. Norah could hear a cow mooing; there was silence, the cow mooed again.

The air was cold, heavy, and pure, except when wind flurries came, clicked branches, and stirred gray lichened shingles on the old roofs. The smoke of the kitchen fire was snatched and whirled away into the all-enveloping grayness; then the wind fell again, and the world was more silent than before.

Norah felt an almost unbearable excitement thrilling in her veins. She was tired, her thoughts were confused and vague, but their sum was exhilaration; here in this gusty country twilight, when the snow was thinned on the hills, and the winter fields and forests at their shabbiest before a storm, a wild elation seized upon her. It was one of the moments in which a soul is reborn; Norah knew then that this land belonged to her and she to it; she must form her life and herself here, this was the beginning of new things, better things—this was her opening door.

She had no choice. The man she had so strangely married had sent her here, and these great stripped trees stirring so uneasily high above her head in the dark, and these stark fields and woods of Foxaway, and the mellowed old sheds and roofs that were blended now into one total of shadow in the fast-gathering gloom, these were her friends—her weapons—her teachers.

A laugh that was like a shout burst from her, and she started at something that moved, close beside her. It was Pauline, with a shawl over her head and a basket in her hand.

"Pauline!"

"You call me?"

"No. What have you got? Eggs?"

"I found eight or nine. They ain't layin' so well, now Huldy's ben too miserable to give 'em hot mash. I'll start in on 'em tomorrow. The last winter I was up here with Dr. Dunsmuir we sold more'n seventeen dollars wuth of eggs."

"You *did!*" Norah exclaimed. Another door opening——

"Yes'm. Them's young hens, they'll do real good on hot mash," Pauline said.

The two women walked down through the fences and paddocks together.

"Your sister says she's going down to New York State on the train tomorrow."

"She doesn't like it here."

"No."

A gale of wind tore by them, and Pauline diverged to say:

"Ef we ain't in for a snow I miss my guess."

"No, do you really think so?" Norah, chilled

for a moment by the thought of Eve, was all enthusiasm again.

"Can't you taste it?" Pauline asked, surprised in her turn. "That flat taste to the air like it hasn't no salt in it."

Presently she said, "You reckon your ma'll go, too?"

"I don't think so. I believe my mother'll stay."

"You were tellin' me you're Mr. Dunsmuir's secretary?"

"He has all the material for a book, and he wanted to get started on it. But then he had a chance to go on this trip with Dr. Sassoon. So he'll start it when he gets back."

"I'd rather stay hum, where it's comfortable and folks can live like Christians!" Pauline commented as they went into the house.

Chapter XII

"EVE *meant to go down to town the second day after our arrival,"* Norah wrote to Barry some weeks later. *"But the aforementioned storm prevented; I'm not going to try again to describe it; suffice it to say that there never in this world was anything so gorgeous. Just one of these little thorny bushes with the red berries on them and the snow weighing down the thorns and the red berries, was enough, as Whitman says, to stagger sextillions of infidels. I'm reading your uncle's Whitman.*

"Eve finally did get to the station on the third day, and about a week later Mother went down for a few days and came back. And Eve came back, and Uncle Rodney came—to remain for life, I think. They complain, but they stay. But as for me, I'm mad—drunk—enthralled with Foxaway. I don't want to go anywhere else, I don't want to miss one minute of it. You can't think how crowded, dry, dull, feverish the city seems, from here.

"We were here a week before I knew that the milk was coming from our *cows. Or cow, at least, for Lily and the 'old heifer' are both dry, and come in triumphantly in May. It is Dolly's milk*

we are enjoying, and what milk—and what cream! The Kleisers get all the milk we don't use, for caring for our cows, but they're going away, so the cows come home next week. The chickens are all laying like mad, and I can sell all the eggs we don't need. I had a man named Ingersoll for a day, chopping wood; he lives up Old Creek way. But I forget you don't know any of these people. I meet them when I'm walking, or at Lassen's, the grocery. Lassen's wife is going to give me an Airedale puppy, 'when they are ready,' as Daisy Ashford says.

"*Your cable arrived, and I am sorry about poor Mr. Cotton's death, but very glad if you are to have the opportunity to go to the Bay of Whales with Dr. Sassoon. That means July, if you come back on the* Ladysmith, *according to the papers, and July will still be glorious here. But every day now is like a miracle, and my heart is too full; it is really too full.*

"*Sometimes the events of December and my answering the advertisement seem like a strange dream, and perhaps we will keep them so. It is impossible for me to get myself back in that mood again and remember how I felt.*

"*Your letter from Hobart asked what we do. I hardly know. The time simply rushes by. Mother and I sleep in the big room off the kitchen, and I usually come out to the kitchen at about seven. That is sunrise now, and the view from the window is lovely. Then we have breakfast; Pauline has hers much earlier. She sleeps over the woodshed, where the steep roof is. She is the comfort of my life, by the way—she got a dollar a day when she went home nights, and gets sixteen dollars a month now, and her mother keeps sending us pies and fresh bread, as if to hold our distinguished patronage.*

"Then after breakfast there are thousands of things to do. We are taking the house room by room and cleaning and straightening and destroying. Your uncle's study is made into a lovely workroom for you, and the parlor is simply heavenly: every good thing in the house is in there.

"Last week we had mild, mild days;—they almost break your heart when they are that way. On one late afternoon walk, coming back from the Kleisers'—their mother had died suddenly just after Bessy, that was their cousin that lived with them, married the man her sister was engaged to before she ran away with Joe Ruddell.

"You see I'm all mixed up in village affairs. Well, anyway, coming back from the Kleisers' I heard the little peepers just going it, down at the pond. It sounded too wonderful. And that day, when the sun was bright, you could see how red the maples were.

"I am not going to sit here all summer idle, waiting for Dr. Sassoon to discover things.

There are many ways I could make money here, and I am going to try one or two. I have told Eve and Elinor that I would take children to board for the summer—or an old lady. And when the cherries come along I can make cherry butter; my mother's mother used to make it, and it is simply delicious.

"All this is a very funny experience to me, and funniest of all is to think how it commenced. Whatever happens, I shall always be glad of it. I say 'whatever happens,' because it is impossible for me to think that the original terms of our contract—you know what I mean—will not be changed. I wish you would think of this; of course you do. It makes me horribly nervous and jumpy sometimes, when I am going off to sleep, to think about—well, December twenty-seventh, and I can only say that I am sure, in any reasonable court, such a thing would not hold for a moment.

"Foxaway is beginning to look lovely. If we could only get Ingersoll to work for more than one day at a time we could get the yard cleared up.

"My money—your money—is holding out well. If you do not leave Hobart until April, you will have this letter before you sail, to wish you a marvelous trip, and to assure you that all is well here. Mother sends her kindest regards with mine."

WIFE FOR SALE

This letter was mailed on the last day of March. On almost every day that followed Norah thought of Barry, and imagined herself writing him more letters with fresh news, exciting news. The apple trees began to bud, and the cherries and plums were balls of snow; there was shy grass, there were dogwoods in bloom. Running water sounded in the dusk. Norah's heart swelled like the blooms themselves; she could hardly endure the miracle that met her at every door and window.

After a while there were lilac and bridal-wreath—too much of them, too deluging a river of bloom, scent, color, singing, and flying sound for human hearts to bear. The skies were all blue, the little river was a sunny mirror between reeds; birds flashed down to it, and flowers bent over and dabbled themselves in its coldness. And still the richness, the prodigality of beauty increased; trees opened wet little fans of green to the moist warm air; lilacs waved in their clean leafy tents; buttercups fringed the roads.

The kitchen windows were wide open now; the upstairs shutters thrown back; sunshine and fresh air streamed through the house, and Mrs. Oliver had a rug and a big chair in the side yard, and sat soaking in sweetness and beauty for the long sunny hours of the spring days. She and Norah moved upstairs and established themselves in one of the largest bedrooms; even Eve came back, discouraged as to job-finding, disgusted with Elinor's complacency and Elinor's husband, and fussed for days over the arrangement of her own room.

"Suppose we went in for jams, Mother, we could probably get one of the big New York firms to handle them. The Foxaway Gooseberry Green. The Foxaway Strawberry Scarlet."

"I thought you were going to try the chicken raising, dear."

"Oh, well! The jams could be a side issue."

"And what about the children you were going to board?" asked Eve.

"Oh, well, children are no trouble."

"And then how about the Foxaway Sunday Lunch, two dollars? That chicken and salad and biscuit lunch——"

"Yes, I know." Norah fell into thought, and Eve said:

"And after all, it isn't your place, you know. Mr. Dunsmuir will be back——"

"He may be delayed. He said, in that letter I had from Hobart, that he wasn't sure Sassoon would want to spend next winter in Ross Bay, and if Sassoon did, he didn't think he, Mr. Dunsmuir, would stay."

"It's funny," Eve said suddenly.

"What's funny?"

"Oh, *you!*—You being here in this old place; you being his secretary without ever having really been his secretary. I should think people would think it was—funny."

"People?"

"Well, everyone."

"Coming just when it did, it seems to me providential," Mrs. Oliver said.

Norah was not listening. In her mind she was formulating various advertisements. Nothing so disfiguring as a highway sign, "Eat Dinner Today at Foxaway." Nothing like that.

But there might be a modest card nailed up in the Post Office or near it, and there might be newspaper advertising in the city. Elinor's boisterous husband was a newspaper advertising man: he could advise her. It would be great fun, when Barry came back, to have some money in the bank; to be able to say to him, "I've proved that a woman *can* make a go of anything she attempts, if she wants to, hard enough."

Besides that, there might be real need. When he had written from Hobart of his extended plan, he had said nothing of money. Norah had rather timidly inquired at the local bank later, feeling that he might have mailed a check to her account there.

Now, early in May, there was still no money, and it behooved her to make some. She put forth feelers. Foxaway Fresh Eggs. Jersey Milk for Sale. Children Boarded for the Summer, or During the Absence of Their Parents. Summer

Boarders. Foxaway Cherry Jam. Country Week-ends a Specialty. Flowers: Let Us Keep You Supplied.

These offers went down to Elinor's husband, Bill Gunther, who found them very funny, but paid for their insertion in the newspaper, which more than atoned for his levity. In June a very rich woman came to see Norah, bringing her two little boys, and a very poor woman came with a small red-headed girl. The rich woman, after an inspection of Foxaway, explained apologetically that she had thought it was all different, more organized, more elaborate and more expensive. Fifty dollars a month was—well, not enough, if Miss Oliver understood what she meant.

The other woman loved everything and all but cried with joy over the bread and milk and prunes that Norah made her share out in the sun at luncheon time. But she had thought—she faltered, she had thought that it was a sort of—well, a place that did not cost so much, that was part supported. Norah, her heart aching with shame and sympathy, asked her what she had expected to pay, and Mrs. Train said hesitantly that—well, last year she had paid five dollars a week.

Barbara Train came flying back at this point from a hasty first examination of Foxaway. "Mother, there is a baby calf—truly, *truly*. And, Mother, baby chickens!" and in the end it had been arranged that Barbara should stay at Foxaway and help with the dishes and be a good girl for Miss Norah at five dollars a week.

Norah wrote Barry a frank, serio-comic letter about her experiments and her difficulties, and sent it to Hobart. She described Barbara, Pauline, her mother's great-lady fineness; she described the astounding courtship and marriage of Uncle Rod and the Widow Taft. She sent her letters to Hobart, feeling that after all Barry might not get them, for no ship would go down to Ross Bay on a mere mail or pleasure trip, after the *Ladysmith* had taken the expedition down in June, and had come back, leaving Sassoon and seven other men, possibly including Barry, on the ice-bound peninsula. But if she were late starting Norah hoped her letter would reach him first. He must gather from what she said that there was need of money.

In early June the newspapers had the story of the departure from Australia. And then on the last day of the month there was other news. The *Ladysmith* had been lost in a heavy storm just outside the ice pack; two Norwegian seamen, sole survivors, had been picked up in one of her lifeboats, after drifting seven hundred miles. Plans for a rescue expedition were already under way, but although every effort to search the Antarctic seas would duly be made, small hopes existed of the survival of Sassoon or of the men who had accompanied him.

Norah, reading the morning paper, stood still in the warm spring sunshine, outside the Post Office, and tried to assimilate this amazing fact. Barry dead! Barry struggling in icy ocean water in the darkness of the night, washed overboard, or sucked in under the sinking *Ladysmith*. It was unthinkable.

Sobered, she walked slowly home. Even knowing that he had faced the danger of death almost hourly on this expedition, somehow she had always felt that Barry would come back; any other possibility had never even occurred to her.

And now he was dead, and fate had given another queer spin to the wheel of Norah's life. Her shadowy wifehood was over before it had begun; no one need ever know now. He had come into the pattern oddly, abruptly, and had played his part, and now he was gone again.

But what about Foxaway? While the village discussed the strangeness and sadness of the death of the last of the Dunsmuirs, Norah mused seriously as to her position here. In the eyes of the world and of her own family, she was merely Mr. Dunsmuir's secretary. Would they let her go peaceably on here at the farm, with Mother and Pauline, or would they tell her that she must move on?

WIFE FOR SALE

And if they did, would she be wise to tell them of the marriage of Barry Dunsmuir—— Norah would stop at this point, shuddering. Oh, she couldn't do that!

What would her mother think, what would everyone think, of the girl who had kept all this a secret, for no reason at all? The world always thought it knew good reasons for such senseless behavior. Norah would be marked for life, here in the village, where she had felt so sheltered and so happy. "She got herself mixed up in some ways with young Dunsmuir," the women in the Post Office would say. "After he died she come out with the whole story, or with what she said was the story! Her mother didn't know one word of it till 'twas all over!"

"Well, what of it?" Norah would demand of herself fiercely, when her uneasy reflections reached this point. "What of it? I don't care what people think! If it's that, or leaving Foxaway, I'll tell everyone everything."

At intervals in the pondering of her own problem, she thought of Barry. It was too bad to go out of life like that, eager and interested and vital as he was! She wondered if he and his adored leader had been together at the end. Had they had time for one shouted message of courage and good-bye before the waters took them? Had Barry had a moment of believing in God, after all? In the sweet June nights, when the warm moonlight streamed across the window sill of her upper bedroom, and made patterns through the pear-tree leaves on the shabby old carpet of the floor, Norah would kneel a few extra seconds at her prayers, remembering Barry.

Chapter XIII

ABOUT a week after the newspaper story of the lost *Ladysmith* two callers appeared at the farm, in the late afternoon peace and beauty: two girls, dainty in flowered chiffons and summer hats, parked a small twinkling car at Norah's gate and came up the garden path, between the phlox and peonies, looking interestedly about them as they came. One was a pale, rather unfriendly looking girl of twenty-eight or -nine; the other, a year or two younger, had ringlets bunched on her neck, and a round, rosy face upon which was a sweet and sentimental expression.

"You're Miss Oliver?" the older girl asked. She sighed, smiled appealingly. "I'm Hazel Dunsmuir," she said, extending her hand. "I'm poor Barry's cousin—his only cousin. Wasn't it terrible?"

"Awful," Norah said, nervously indicating the basket chairs under the big elm. They all sat down.

"This is Miss Swann, Miss Oliver, another person of whom Barry was very fond," Hazel said.

"*Please*——" Miss Swann said faintly, looking away. Her eyes watered.

"I think he had a premonition of it!" Miss Dunsmuir said boldly.

"Barry?" Norah asked involuntarily. Instead of answering, Hazel looked at her in surprise.

"Did you know him so well?" she asked abruptly.

Norah was scarlet, but she smiled.

"The newspapers," she responded with composure, "make one feel as if one knew all about him."

"I see," Hazel said. "You were his secretary, weren't you?"

"I was to be—I hadn't really started. He engaged me in December, and then he went away on the twenty-seventh——"

"I know when he went away," Hazel put in neatly. "I was the closest relative he had!"

Norah making no comment upon this, she added:

"We're at Glen Garden for the summer, and I hoped to see a great deal of Barry!"

"He loved this place," Norah observed mildly.

"Oh, why wouldn't he?" Lucille Swann said emotionally. "He talked of it continually." She wiped her eyes, looked away again.

"You knew," Hazel began directly, her eyes on Norah, "that he left it to me?"

Norah's heart sank. Foxaway, with its elms, its lanes and fences, its silvered old roof and square-paned windows, was hers no longer. No, but she—she was Barry's legal wife, after all. Hazel knew nothing of that claim——

Her confused thoughts kept her silent.

"I asked him for it outright," Hazel confessed frankly. "I love the old place—it's the family homestead, and we're all *devoted* to it!"

"You wouldn't rent it, I suppose?" Norah asked hesitantly.

"Not for five hundred a month!" Hazel answered with a triumphant laugh.

"I've grown fond of it, too," Norah admitted. "I've got my mother here, and we've been taking it, room by room—clearing it out. We feel as if it were home."

"I'm sorry," Hazel said politely, stiffly, with a touch of triumph again in her voice.

"There are books—family letters and diaries here," Norah went on. "We've been straightening it all out."

"My mother and I intend to put everything in order," Hazel countered quickly. "If you'll just leave things as they are——" she added, significantly. Norah's ready color flamed again.

"Barry—Mr. Dunsmuir had asked me to get the place ready for him," she said, with a stiffness equal to Hazel's own. Hazel was ready for her with a firm, light, "Ah, well, since he's not coming back——" and Norah felt that she hated her.

"Hazel, the dreams—the dreams—the dreams!" Miss Swann put in at this point. Her sensitive eyes were again filled with tears; she was looking off into the greenness, the rich flowery beauty of the gardens and the surrounding woods and hills; her hands were clasped, her voice filled with longing.

"Ah, you poor thing!" Hazel said affectionately.

"One means to be—game about it," Lucille Swann managed to enunciate faintly.

"You *are* game, you're being a wonderful sport about it!" Hazel assured her warmly. She turned to Norah, spoke with a touch of crisp authority, as she got to her feet. "We'll be going now, Miss Oliver," she said. "This makes Lucille here feel too badly. But you'll let me know, at the hotel in Glen Gardner, what your own plans are, won't you? Mother and I don't want to hurry you, but we would like, of course, to take possession as soon as we can!"

Standing, Miss Swann had clasped her hands on her breast.

"To think of the might-have-been, Hazel!" she breathed.

Hazel put a comforting arm about her, turned to Norah in explanation.

"I suppose you knew that my cousin Barry and Miss Swann were to have been married this summer?" she asked, in her careless, superior manner. "That's why—all this is too much for her!"

"Going to be married?" Norah said, with the world going around her in lazy, dizzying circles.

Lucille herself answered, with her sad, brave smile.

"We cared for each other—oh, dearly! I was to have been his wife—this was to have been our home!" she said.

Chapter XIV

NORAH stood looking at her for a long minute, while the summer day hummed, shone, sang, and buzzed sweetness about them like a symphony. She was very pale; she made an effort to speak; could not speak.

Both the other girls were visibly affected by her emotion; Lucille began softly to cry, and her friend lowered her gently into the chair she had just vacated.

"Sit down, dear," Hazel said.

After a moment they all sat down, looking at each other soberly. Little Barbara Train, six years old, came through the green light of the grape arbor and wedged her small person into the chair with Norah. Norah put her arm about her, but her gaze never left Hazel's face; afterward Hazel and Lucille could tell each other quite without exaggeration that if there had been nothing between Barry and his secretary, at least Miss Oliver had turned ashen white at the news of his engagement, and that her manner had been dazed for many minutes.

"I didn't know he was engaged," Norah finally enunciated.

Lucille nodded, touching her handkerchief to her eyes. Hazel spoke.

"He was at our house last autumn when he got back. That was just after my uncle's death, here at Foxaway. And Lucille was with us too, weren't you, dear?"

"We were terribly happy," Lucille admitted frankly. "And tell her—" she went on, a little incoherently, "about—you—you know—now —now——"

"She's in terror for fear the newspapers will get hold of it!" Hazel explained. "She doesn't want anyone to know!"

"I couldn't bear it!" Miss Swann whispered, leaning her head back against the grape arbor and shutting her eyes.

"Don't worry, they'll not get it," Hazel assured her. She looked about the arbor. "Aren't all these tables new?" she asked.

"I had Ingersoll, a carpenter here, make them," Norah answered. "We serve—we're going to serve—we were going to serve!—chicken lunches here on Sundays."

"Not at Foxaway!" Miss Dunsmuir said sharply.

"Well, we haven't really begun yet. We had four people last Sunday," Norah went on, "but they ate our dinner; we hadn't expected them!"

"But not at Foxaway!"

The tone of horror edged Norah's own tone with resentment when she spoke again.

"I wrote Mr. Dunsmuir at Hobart that it seemed a shame not to use the place."

"But he surely didn't agree to turning it into a roadhouse?"

Norah looked at the other girl levelly; her tone was level.

"No; he didn't agree to turning it into a roadhouse."

There was a brief pause. Then Hazel said:

"I thought you were doing secretarial work for Mr. Dunsmuir?"

"I was to, originally. But then he was invited to go with Dr. Sassoon——"

"Naturally, I know that," Hazel interpolated haughtily. "But hadn't you been his secretary before? Hadn't you the notes for his book?"

"No. I only met Mr. Dunsmuir in December."

"Oh, you hadn't worked for him before he went on the last trip?"

Suddenly, inexplicably, Norah felt frightened. The effect of these direct, hostile questions was to unnerve her. She felt confusedly that there was no use lying about the situation; if Barry was never going to come back these people would discover everything, sooner or later. Lucille afraid of newspapers, indeed! Norah could feel their hot breath on her own bare skin: they would make the most of the story of a lost explorer, secretly engaged to one girl, secretly wed to another!

And even while she talked to these visitors, in her mind she was busily explaining to someone authoritative—someone legal:

"No, your honor, I had seen him only those few times. Through a newspaper advertisement, your honor. No, sir, I had said that I would marry anyone who would support my mother——"

Aloud she said: "Mr. Dunsmuir advertised for a—he put an advertisement in the paper, and I answered it."

"It doesn't sound one bit like Barry!" his cousin said, as if she were thinking aloud. "There were plenty of secretaries at the Coates & Goldman office, I know that, for they had to let me out; I worked there one whole winter eighteen months ago."

Norah said nothing; her face was red.

"Are we going to take our supper up to the spring?" little Barbara asked eagerly.

"We surely are. Go get some tomatoes, Barbara, big firm ones, and put them in the ice house so they'll be nice and cold. And put on your hat before you go out to that hot vegetable garden."

"It wasn't 'Mrs. Oliver,' was it?" Hazel asked.

"I? No, Miss Oliver," Norah said. But her face flamed again; it was maddening, it was humiliating, to face these insolent questions. "Barbara isn't my child, if you mean that," she said. "Her mother is a naval lieutenant's widow who works in Phillipsburg. She's left Barbara with me for the summer."

"But I haven't asked my mother's question," Hazel said, after a pause. "She feels that after this—this shocking accident to the poor old *Ladyslipper*—was it? *Ladysmith,* I mean, there'll be all sorts of legal procedures—that sort of thing. You see, my uncle, Dr. Dunsmuir, died only last year, and his estate—much less poor Barry's—isn't settled yet. And Mother felt that she'd like to know what your plans are."

Norah, roused to retaliation, faced her steadily.

"I'm employed by Mr. Dunsmuir. He especially wanted me to be here, to get the place in order, and wait for him," she said coldly.

"Yes, but now that—unfortunately, he's not coming back."

"We don't *know* he's not coming back," Norah said. "After all, the *Ladysmith* carried four lifeboats."

"Oh, but, my dear!" Hazel protested patiently.

"I think I'd *feel* it, if Barry was coming back!" Lucille said in a sleepwalker's tone. Her friend, they were all standing now, again put a bracing arm about her.

"Ah, no, dear; ah, no!" Hazel said. "I think we must go now," she added coldly.

And immediately afterward they climbed into the smart little roadster and were gone. Norah stood looking after them for a long, long time. Then she turned and went into the farmhouse, and the mellowed old halls and rooms received her into their shadowy summer peace and beauty and quieted her soul.

The kitchen was in spotless order; the dining room shaded and empty. Subdued light battened at the drawn shades of the parlor, and Norah could see the walnut chairs, the old rug, the crystal candlesticks, and the dim portraits over the mantel, all with the quiver of outlawed summer light trembling upon them like pond water. Her own chair, with its decorous antimasassar and footstool; Barbara's little rocker; Mother's chair. Her books; she was never done with arranging them, straightening them, exploring them. A great jar of peonies was on the table; another of mixed garden flowers, blue and red and yellow and white, on the old square piano.

Home—home—home! She had made this place; she had rescued it from oblivion and decay. The deepest fibers of her being were knit to it; she could not imagine life without Foxaway.

Engaged to Barry indeed, that sentimental idiot of a girl with a snood around her hair! She had taken off her hat in the arbor, and Norah somehow had felt that Barry never would have liked this lackadaisical young person with her velvet snood!

Or had he really liked her, and then changed his mind, and with that dreadful incisive logic of his determined to marry for other reasons than a mere fancy, bred of a house party——

They would never know now. Unless, of course, even the icy Southern ocean had failed to conquer Barry's crisp resourcefulness and iron determination. He might be alive somewhere.

Life began to seem complicated. It wasn't that Hazel's intrusion, Hazel's half threats, had really worried her, but it was disturbing to have so many uncertainties on her mind. Her claim on Foxaway, and her secret, and finances, were all problems that she must face alone. Her bank account, for example, must eternally be balanced against a mental litany that ran, "Pauline's sixteen dollars, and about five a week at Lassen's—but there's the calf money, he hasn't given me that yet, and boarding the Van Vleets' horses while they were up at the Lake, and Barbara's twenty——"

However, even though vague, this last usually came out satisfactorily enough, for there were many small avenues of revenue in summer, and her expenses were ludicrously low. Pauline took the family washing in her stride, as it were, and there was fruit, and there were berries, and corn and tomatoes and milk and cream and eggs and broilers in embarrassing plenty, to reduce the grocery bill. Pauline was always "putting up" a few currants or crab-apples, and always "salting down" butter and eggs against the winter. She would quite casually make three pies instead of one, and report later to Norah, "I sold two of them pies over to the hotel, Miss Oliver—one of them ladies in the cottages took the both of 'em! I put the fifty cents into the cup there."

No, if Norah never seemed to have any money, on the other hand, country folk needed little.

Her continually dashed hopes of a business success occasioned more serious thought. Norah puzzled and wondered over her experiences. Nothing that she attempted ever came out the way it did in magazine stories or books. Wasn't it really possible to make a living, except in an office, under orders, as a cog in a big machine?

The Sunday chicken dinners of Foxaway had never been widely advertised, and when July had passed with only a record of one party of four, Norah had rather abandoned that idea. But immediately afterward, on the first August Sunday, in a deluging rain, seventeen hilarious motorists had arrived in five separate parties, all demanding dinner. On this occasion Elinor and Bill also had come up from town unexpectedly, and the simple Sunday fare had been consumed to the last crumb before the first customer appeared. Bill had thought this so funny that Norah, red-cheeked, politely directing her patrons to the inn up at the Lake, had felt that she could slay him.

Earlier, she and Pauline had put up two hundred jars of cherry butter, and that they had advertised. It had sold well, too, for a week. Then the buyers had begun to return to Foxaway Farm in the exact order of their original appearance, bearing glasses of the sugared red horror and demanding explanations. The explanations had had to take the form of refunding, and Norah and Pauline, after some further hot and sticky experiments in the "lean-to," had thrown the whole bubbling, odorous mass of the cherry jam away.

Undiscouraged, a few days later Norah went up to some of the big Lake hotels and was permitted to display cards: "Mending Carefully Done." "Birthday Cakes for Parties." "Companions Supplied for Invalids or Elderly Persons." "Honey." "Garden Flowers."

All through that first summer at Foxaway these offers received no attention whatsoever. If any casual visitor at the farm was for a moment interested, the inevitable "Give me your telephone number," and Norah's regretful, "We haven't electricity at Foxaway," ended the matter once and for all.

Barbara remained her only boarder, and although Norah's brain was as fertile as ever in suggestions: "We could have a wonderful scout camp here—we could give children's parties here—we could have a convalescent home here!" somehow nothing ever materialized.

Then there were other anxieties. Norah knew that she might be summarily evicted any day. Barry's aunt, the rich Mrs. Dunsmuir, came majestically to the farm one hot August afternoon, and her conversation with Norah was painful for them both.

"You've done wonders for the old place," Mrs. Dunsmuir began graciously, after the rather strained preliminaries. "Dear old Foxaway! We used all to be here in my husband's lifetime, when Barry was a boy in college. He loved the place so!"

"We've only cleaned, really," Norah said. "Pauline and I have just done one thing after another——"

"Your sister?"

"Well, my sister Evelyn has helped, too. But Pauline is just a girl from the town."

"Was that my poor nephew's—dear unfortunate boy!—was that his idea?"

"Was what?"

"Was it dear Barry's idea to put the old place in shape?"

"Oh, yes: he wanted to do some writing here."

"He was going to live here?"

"He said so."

"You knew he was going to marry my daughter Hazel's dear friend, Lucille Swann?"

"They told me."

"The newspapers have got her story, poor child, and they have blazoned it, trumpeted it, over their wretched first pages."

"Oh, did she tell them?"

"No," the older woman said severely, "she didn't tell them. They have their own contemptible ways of finding things out! Nothing is sacred—nothing safe."

"I don't see the papers," Norah said slowly, thinking.

"Well, they had the whole story, her pictures, everything. The poor child is prostrated! His death, of course, is a terrible shock to us all."

"He may not be dead."

"Nonsense!" Mrs. Dunsmuir said sharply. "And that brings me to my errand," she went on. "Frankly, may I know what your plans are, so that I may form my own?"

"My plans?"

"We're very anxious to come here, Miss

Oliver, my daughter and poor Lucille and I. The place—we've seen the will—is Hazel's. It's a Dunsmuir property, of course. Barry spoke of it last autumn when he was at my house! 'I'm leaving the farm to Hazel, I don't know what she'll do with it: it isn't worth taxes!' he said. Poor fellow, poor fellow. It was only a sort of joke then, but it is like a prophecy now, and Hazel feels—we all do—that Barry would want us here—would want our hands to be handling his books, our wishes to be respected in regard to——" She stopped as her eloquence tightened her throat and brought tears to her eyes.

"But you see," Norah interpolated, "he sent me here. I'm in his employ. I had my instructions."

"Certainly not to turn the place into an infant farm and roadhouse!"

"No, not to do that. But to take care of it until he came back."

"My dear child, you don't think that rescue ship is going to find him!"

"I don't think anything. If it doesn't, I suppose he'll be officially dead: that's what the papers seem to think, anyway."

"Well, exactly."

"But until they do," said Norah, "I think I ought to stay here. I really do."

"Perhaps you'll let me be the judge of that.

After all, in situations as—as sad, as unfortunate as this one, the family—the family has its rights."

"My family has, I know!" Norah conceded with a cheerful laugh. "I don't somehow feel that he and Dr. Sassoon are dead at all," she went on; "they *can't* be. And if he came back I'd feel that I had broken my contract . . ."

After a while Mrs. Dunsmuir left, vanquished for the moment, at least, but the effect of the conversation was to make Norah uneasy. Lucille's engagement to the lost explorer was common property; the tabloids, the pictorials were making the most of it. Now was not the moment to announce a secret marriage to the same man.

And after all, the real sum and climax of her troubles was that she was married to Barry Dunsmuir. All very well to talk of annulling and "not going through with it," and to say that there could easily be some arrangement made, it must be easy to slip out of such an affair, but the stark truth remained: she was married to him. That was on her record for life, whatever she did, her swift and secret marriage to a man she hardly knew, who had immediately departed on a long and dangerous journey, leaving her to face the music as best she might. She had never had an opportunity to love him, she had barely liked him; he might, upon his return, prove to be completely hateful to her; they might actively dislike each other. And still she would be married to him, and all her casuistry and courage could not wriggle her free.

Chapter XV

DELIVERANCE from at least one of these burdens came unexpectedly on a certain exquisite September day some two weeks after Mrs. Dunsmuir's visit. Norah, flashing out to the porch upon one of her endless morning errands, discovered a majestic gray-headed old man comfortably seated there, fanning himself with a palm-leaf fan.

"Did you wish dinner?" she asked, with a panicky thought that included the fact that it was Monday, wash day for Pauline, and that very little prepared food was in the house after Sunday.

"Do you serve dinner?" the visitor asked, surprised.

"I do everything!" But Norah was regarding him in sudden interest now, and changed the subject by saying abruptly, "You—I know you. I'm afraid I've forgotten—no, I haven't. Isn't it Judge Bailey?"

"Why, God bless me," the man said bewilderedly, turning to scrutinize her more keenly. "Do we know each other?"

"Mr. Dunsmuir took me to your office last December. You were in the office, in the office of Coates & Goldman, last December, when I was there with Barry Dunsmuir."

"Why, so I was—so I was!" he said, enlightened. "So *you* are the Miss Oliver I've heard so much about! And I never identified you with the girl who came in with Barry—poor Barry. Sad thing! Sad thing!"

"Have you heard so much about me?" Norah asked curiously.

"His aunt—his cousin, the Dunsmuirs—very old friends of mine," the old man explained significantly. "They've been making a good deal of fuss, in one way and another, about your staying here."

"They both came to see me about it, the mother and the daughter."

"Yes, well—yes, well——" Judge Bailey began fretfully. He rubbed his head. "They're in a great hurry to settle up the poor boy's affairs!" he said.

"But how can they do that if he isn't dead?"

"They can't legally. But I suppose the presumption—the presumption is that he *is* dead."

"Well, I know——" Norah said, and paused on the stubborn phrase. "They want me to get out of here," she said, "and he wanted me to stay here. He intended to live here, you know. He was going to write a book."

"He was going to marry this nice little Swann girl—Hazel's friend."

"Had he told you so?" Norah asked.

A quizzical smile narrowed the old man's eyes.

"Didn't you see that story in the papers?"

"Oh, she told me so, for that matter," Norah said.

"And you didn't believe it?"

Norah made no answer. She was thinking.

"Well," said Judge Bailey, rubbing his head again, "it struck me as odd too. It seemed very strange. Very unlike the boy, and I knew him well! It didn't seem to me he would ever marry anyone."

"He wouldn't marry two women at once, anyway," Norah submitted, with sudden color in her face.

There was a silence. The old man looked at her steadily.

"You and he were engaged, my dear?" he presently inquired respectfully.

"Not engaged. Married," Norah said.

Another pause, during which they continued to look full at each other.

"Mr. Barry Dunsmuir married?"

"We were married on December twenty-seventh, the day before he went away."

After a while Judge Bailey said several times in succession, "You and Barry *married?*" and Norah said, "Yes," each time. The old man took out his big fine handkerchief and wiped his forehead, for the September day was warm.

"Why, I had no idea of his intention to marry," he said. "His will—it was filed in our office—made no mention of a wife! But, to be sure, that was some months before he sailed."

"He said something—that last day, of changing his will, or making a new will, I remember."

"He didn't. My gracious!" ejaculated the old man, "this is a complication. You and Barry, eh? Had known each other some time, eh?"

"Only a short time. Only a week or ten days, really. It was—it wasn't—the usual sort of—engagement," explained Norah, flushing brightly, fumbling for words. "He—he isn't—wasn't like anyone else about it. I was—well, we were having hard times, horrible times, my mother and sister and brother and I, and we lived in a dreadful place; I was—desperate. Keith—my brother—had lost his job, and I had lost mine, and it—it interested Barry. It was like a problem to him, something he could solve."

"Exactly! That was the boy!" the old man agreed, watching her intently, nodding his gray head.

"He said he didn't believe the usual love-making was necessary—or at least that it was any sign of a happy marriage."

"You met him—where?"

"He answered an advertisement of mine."

"Barry did?"

"Well, it wasn't the usual thing; not as a stenographer, exactly. It was more that I was—I was up against it, I said I would do anything—anything honorable, that is—for someone to help my mother, take some of the load. Keith, my brother, was in love, and he couldn't think of anything but himself and Anne, and my sister Evelyn was just nineteen, and Mother sick——"

"You said you would even marry such a man, eh?"

"Well," Norah spoke hesitatingly, "if I liked him."

Judge Bailey's face brightened into a smile.

"And you did like Barry?"

"It wasn't so much that, as that he was—*eager* to try the experiment. He said he wanted just that—a wife, companionship. He doesn't like cities and crowds, and he said he didn't want the responsibility of keeping house. He told me that his uncle had left him this place—Foxaway——"

Norah stopped. She glanced up at the bulk of the old farmhouse above and behind her.

"I love it!" she said, in a low voice, as if she spoke only to herself. "I've never loved anything so much. It seems the place where I belong, like a part of me. I suppose there are other old places round here that are just as wonderful, but none of them would ever be Foxaway. I've been happy here, without any money or friends or excitement; it satisfies me."

The old man was thinking.

"But then this other girl, Lucille—Lucille Swann. What about her? D'you figure it that Barry made love to the girl in October—he was with the Dunsmuirs in October—and then just dropped her flat?"

"I don't think he ever paid her the slightest attention." Norah smiled for the first time.

"Don't!" echoed the old man, with a ludicrous falling of the jaw.

"I don't know anything about it, of course. But she never told the other girl, Hazel, anything about her engagement until—well, until there was reason to think Barry wouldn't come back."

"Ha!" ejaculated Judge Bailey. "I'm staying over here at the Lake with my daughter," he presently added, "and Mrs. Dunsmuir asked me to have a talk with you. I'm poor Barry's executor, of course."

"They want me to get out?"

"They had some idea of spending the rest of the month and October here; there are books here, old family things——"

He paused.

"But this news of yours," he went on, rubbing his chin thoughtfully, "this places a different—

a different complexion on the whole thing. Married, eh? Well, you—you surprise me!"

"My own mother doesn't know," said Norah.

"Your own mother? But then," pursued the Judge, "was it the idea that when poor Barry did come back, you and he should announce it?"

"He was hardly sure that he would go at all, Judge, when we—decided it." Norah hesitated. "His going has made it all difficult," she said. "If he had come back, I don't know quite what we should have done. It—our getting married, was a sort of dare, an impulse——"

"Barry having had this idea that marriage could be arranged that way, in the European way, on a perfectly common-sense basis," the old man formulated it, as she fell silent, "advertised for a stenographer, and then picked the one he liked, and put his—his proposal to her?"

"Not quite that!" Norah said, uncomfortably, with a little nervous laugh. "It—it really came from me. I don't think he would have thought of it. I said that to have Mother taken care of, and to have a home, I'd marry—oh, not anyone, but any man who—who impressed me as being good and honest. I said I'd make a home for him and take care of him and his children."

"Why, my daughter Rosa saw something in the paper like that months ago. A letter, I think it was."

"Yes. I wrote that. And Barry put a personal in that same paper, a few days later, and we met that way."

The Judge fell into deep thought, his fine old mouth half smiling.

"Yes, that's exactly what Barry would do, that's the kind of thing that would have appealed to him," he said. "But he was a fine fellow," he said warmly. "He was a fine fellow, he was one of the best!"

"Afterward, when he had the chance to go off with Dr. Sassoon," Norah pursued, warming herself to her companion's sympathy, "it all seemed so much less of a joke—our marriage, I mean. I came up here." Her loving eyes wandered over the rich beauty of the old farm: the deep-foliaged trees, the mellow shadows on the farm buildings and the fences, the woods and rolling hills beyond. Everything was wrapped in silence and fragrance and peace in the early autumn afternoon.

"It's surely a pretty old place," the Judge said.

"It's changed me, everything about me," Norah said, not looking at him, speaking as if she were merely thinking aloud. "I've cooked and washed and raked and pruned, I've painted and sewed and gathered eggs and mixed food for chickens and cows, here; I've washed dishes and churned milk and ironed handkerchiefs—

I've *lived* here. Mother and Barbara and I have our suppers out here under the maples every night. Each one of us gets what she wants and brings it out on a tray, with a book—or without a book. I've come down here from my bed, moonlight nights, and just stood out here, looking around—loving it."

The old man cleared his throat.

"Well," he said, "I see no reason why you shouldn't stay here. Lacking—ahem!—direct heirs, this place would revert to you as the widow."

Norah laughed forlornly.

"It sounds so—*awful,*" she said. "But then, you see, Judge," she went on, "Mrs. Dunsmuir claims that under the will this place was left to Hazel."

"I see, I see," he agreed in a puzzled tone, scraping his chin again. "But in that case," he added, "you will have money enough to make some other arrangement for yourself and your mother."

Norah looked at him in surprise.

"How do you mean?"

"Why, if this relief expedition fails, as it probably will fail, you will come in for a good deal of property, my dear. Barry was by no means a rich man, but his uncle's estate——"

A startled look came into the girl's eyes.

"I never thought of that!"

WIFE FOR SALE

After a while the Judge said:

"Suppose I put it this way to Mrs. Dunsmuir? You are in Barry's employ, and his directions were that you were to live here. You are perfectly justified in doing so at least until the courts are satisfied that he is not going to return. Just as soon as anything definite about Barry is decided, then you make known that you are his wife, and your claim of course is recognized."

"That would be wonderful!" Norah approved, with a flash of gray eyes.

"Wiser, I think, than to give this marriage to the papers, just now, when everyone is talking about him."

"Oh, much wiser."

The old man got to his feet, held out a friendly hand; his eyes were very kind as he looked down at Norah.

"My dear, you have had a strange story."

"It seems to me strange," Norah said.

"I am sorry for Barry. He was a lonely fellow. And no man could want a finer home than this one, or a—" he bowed, a little at a loss for words, "or a happier future," he said.

"Oh, thank you!" Norah said, blinking suddenly wet eyelashes, trying to laugh. "It all— came out so differently," she went on lamely, "so differently from what we expected!"

He looked at her keenly.

"But you did—like him, eh?"

Norah's face flamed.

"I don't know," she admitted honestly. "I've felt terribly grateful to him," she said.

The old man went to his waiting car, and Norah came out from the kitchen with an old lard tin filled to the brim with great ripe blackberries, and a small wrapped jar.

"These are the Foxaway blackberries; you've never seen such beauties!" she said. "And this is some of our cream. Would you and Mrs. Bailey like them for your supper?"

"Why, thank you. Mrs. Bailey and my daughter will come over and thank you themselves," the Judge said. "I hope you two girls will be friends."

Norah stood looking after him until the last black twinkle of the car vanished at the turn of the road. Then she walked back from the gate to the house, stopping to pick a spray of velvet sweet dark wallflower, stopping again to look up at the splendid star-shaped leaves of the mighty maple that brushed against the bedroom windows.

Mother was asleep, up there, and Pauline, who always selected the most broiling hour of the hottest possible day to feel energetic and fresh, with wet-combed hair and stiff percale dress and sunbonnet, had taken Barbara fishing. Before it would be necessary to start supper trays, a delicious time of leisure stretched ahead of Norah; it was not yet five o'clock. But the strong sun was descending on the western hill, and shadows were lengthening. Bees shot across the garden, and in one shaft of light a column of little flies was weaving madly. The chickens were beginning to trail slowly to the barns from their favorite dust bath in the shade of the elms by the fence.

This was the hour of hours to walk up to the spring pool. Every inch of the way would be interesting, and once there she could have an icy drink, or an icy peach, and sit on the rock, and look off across all the world.

But she had not gone ten feet before the sound of a motor behind her made her turn about. A smart yellow roadster was coming up the road under the big trees, and while she watched, it was stopped on the drive by the side door, and a young man sprang out of it. A tall, square young man in white, with no hat on his shining light brown hair. He called to her:

"Norah!"

Norah went toward him, smiling vaguely. Who on earth——

Then suddenly the blood left her heart in a rush; came back with a rush, and she felt her pulses begin to pound.

"David!" she said. "David Howard!"

"Norah!" the boy said delightedly. "What fun!"

"But—David!" she stammered. The boy was delighted with her confusion.

"Surprise, hey?"

"Surprise!"

He laughed joyously; he had bent impulsively, at their first meeting, to put a light kiss on her forehead; he was still holding her hands.

"But how'd you find me?" She mustn't be a fool—she mustn't be a fool——

"I've been here three days, at the hotel—on my vacation. My cousins the Parker Potters—you've heard of them?"

Everyone had heard of them, of course. Yachts, Palm Beach, Europe, débutante parties, Junior League, opera boxes—that summed up the Parker Potters. Norah nodded.

"Well, they always come up here—they practically run the place. Norah, this is keen! I've been seeing your little signs at the hotel—it was only today that someone said something about 'Norah Oliver,' and I came right over! Listen, why haven't you a phone?"

"Don't want one."

"Oh, nonsense, you'll have to have one. Norah, isn't this fun? Mad at me?"

"Mad at you?" With just the right innocent air, the right crinkle to her brows as she looked at him. "Why?"

"You know darned well why!" But he was laughing; he was not afraid of her anger. "Gee," he said fervently, as if he thought aloud, "I'm glad to see you! I—am—glad—to—see—you! How's everything?"

"Wonderful!"

So far so good, but her voice would shake, and she felt the color in her face. David again—David talking to her again!

It made her feel a little dizzy. She had liked him so much a year ago—so much more than was wise or dignified or happy. She had dreamed of him, prayed about him. She had pocketed her pride when David Howard had seemed to forget her; had telephoned his mother, had made excuses to send him notes, had tried in every way a girl could—indeed, in many ways she hated to remember now—to remind him of her existence and her affection. She had schooled herself for this moment of meeting again, schooled herself to coldness and reproof, and as often she had melted into forgiveness, into tenderness, just because she liked him and needed him.

She reached blindly for her resolution and courage now. She had on her blue chiffon, fortunately; it had been Elinor's, and Elinor couldn't wear last year's clothes this year, and so its delicate softness and shadowy blueness had been cut down for Norah. And, fortunately again, she had dampened her hair and combed it severely into ripples and fishtails against her browned skin before coming downstairs an hour ago for the unexpected encounter with Judge Bailey.

"David, it's ages since I've seen you," she said, with banality. It was not much, but at least it was better than to burst into tears and cling to him.

"Well, is that all I get?" he said laughing. And her heart—her fool heart, she called it fiercely to herself, began to flutter again. "No, but let's sit down, Norah," David said, "and talk it over. There's something I've got to say to you, and I've been wanting to say it for a long time."

"Come up to the spring pool, it's only two minutes' walk. I was going there anyway to get some peaches."

They walked along together, and David said enthusiastically,

"What a swell old place! Isn't it Dunsmuir's place? Didn't they say so at the hotel?"

"Yes; I was his secretary."

"Some place. See in the paper this morning that they think they've found him?"

The green beauty of Foxaway swept about her giddily. Norah managed to walk on.

"Did the paper say that?"

"Didn't you see it? The radio announced it

too, someone said. No, they haven't found him. But the rescue ship sent a radio that they'd picked up one of the other lifeboats, with six men in it, and they said Dr. Sassoon—I don't remember. But, anyway, they'd all been together until about a month ago."

Norah sat down on the great stone that served as a seat beside the spring. Her eyes were dazed, fixed on far space. Under the tan her face had grown pale.

"You're prettier than ever, Norah," David said. "Do you know that I'm crazy about you?"

Chapter XVI

THEY sat by the spring and talked, and the glorious dying summer day about them was only a reflection, an extension of the heaven that was in their own hearts.

David had his big arm laid along the rocky ledge behind the great dry mossy boulder where they sat; their feet were deep in ferns and bracken and the crisp carpet of last year's leaves. Below them the gracious lines of the hills and the great trees fell away to the village, asleep in sunset. Nearer were the silvered farm buildings, and the elms and maples and fruit trees, and the furred roof and magnificent roof line of the farmhouse. Between the high attic windows on the chimney side a great iron "S" had been sunk into the bricks and plaster; pear-tree shadows flickered over the soft discolored clapboards that had once been white but that were mellowed now to pearly gray.

"I've had the rottenest year I ever had!" David said.

"Oh, David, why?"

"Oh, everything. I took a six months' leave, you know."

"From college!"

"Yep. I was going to be flunked out. I'm coaching now until Christmas. Four of us are up here with a coach."

"Near here?"

"Over in Morristown."

"Why, David, *that's* not very far!" the girl said, pleased.

"That's what I was thinking. How long do you stay?"

"I'm going to stay right along."

"Not through the winter?"

"Oh, yes; through the winter. I love the winter."

David was looking down at her cheek, his own brown cheek, upon which the skin was stretched tightly, very close.

"I had forgotten what black eyelashes you had, Norah!"

"The better to see you with."

"And I had forgotten that you have much too much mouth, and it's much too red. I never saw such a mouth!"

"I'm sorry you don't like it," said Norah.

He did not move his eyes from their oblique study of her flushed and happy face.

"Unfortunately I like it very much," he said, in a low tone.

"Unfortunately?" she said lightly. But her voice was trembling.

"Norah, how did we ever happen to get away from each other?"

"I don't know."

Both their voices were lowered now, though there was no one to overhear, in all the deepening beauty of the orchard and the garden.

"I thought you had forgotten all about me, David."

"I never forgot about you. I was worried, and my father was raising hell with me, and I had to study like mad. And even while I was working I'd be—mentally telephoning to you. And then I'd think, 'No, she's downtown now,' or 'No, she's probably out at a movie.' Or I'd say to myself, 'I'll see her tomorrow, that's Sunday, and that'll be better than any telephoning.'"

After a while he said, "Did you care?"

"Not seeing you? Yes—I did for a while."

He was silent for a moment; then said,

"I am probably the rottenest human being in existence!"

"Oh, don't say that, David!" Norah objected mildly.

"No, I mean it. I really mean it. I get started at one thing and I'm *good,* and then I branch off——

"The old man gave me some terrible call-downs about it last spring. He got awfully soured on me. I can't seem, Norah," David went on, "I can't seem to concentrate except on one thing at a time—I'm *rotten*."

She said he was not rotten at all, and could presently go on to say that last year had been horrid anyway, and that really was why she minded his not coming to see her any more: Elinor, her sister, had eloped for one thing, and Keith, her brother, and his Anne had been all over the place, and Mother had been ill. And then the job-losing had begun, and altogether she had felt horrible all year. . . .

They talked together, absorbed, ecstatic, completely happy in being united again; Norah's square, firm hand was tight in David's; their eyes but a few inches apart.

"I went out to your house—oh, it's months ago, and that cross-eyed janitor's wife told me you had all moved up into New Jersey. It sounded crazy!"

"We came up in January."

"But weren't you snowed in?"

"We actually were, for a few days—with no running water, and nothing but kerosene lamps! But after that it was all fun!"

"Norah, there's nobody like you!" David said.

He was a tall boy, with fair hair and light blue eyes that looked odd in his Indian-brown face. It was a nice face, lean and intelligent and pleasant. Norah liked everything about it: big nose, big jaw, high cheek bones; and about his big lean hands and rather lanky, loose-jointed person.

When he walked down to his car she went with him, and Mrs. Oliver, enjoying the cooling air of the side yard, welcomed him affectionately and asked him to dinner.

David could not stay because he was his cousin's guest at the hotel and could not disappoint her. He went away, and Norah, going into the close hot gloom of the house, stuffy after the airy out-of-doors, reflected that there was a certain dignity, a certain great advantage, in being able to ask your friends to share a meal with you without eternally estimating food. Even though supper tonight was only salad and berries and milk and cornbread, it was pleasant to know that there was plenty of it, and that a guest would not have given anyone a moment's worry or annoyance.

Her heart, her very soul, seemed glowing like the glowing garden tonight. The world was all magic: the sunset and the twilight, and that mingling of twilight and moonlight that sometimes turned the farm into fairyland. It would not be quite dusk tonight until eight, when the moon would rise, big and red and near, over the haycocks in the eastern meadow, and its golden light would meet the last shafts of the dimming glory of the west.

Norah ate her supper thoughtfully; she

seemed to be smiling inside, somehow. David was back in her life, eh?—And so delightfully back! No girl alive could have wished a prettier setting than the great trees and the blazing garden, and the shadows up at the spring pool, and she had had Elinor's chiffon on too—and a shade hat. She had looked as well as she ever could look, and that was all one ever desired of life. And, obviously, it had been enough for David. Norah knew when a man was attracted, was eager, was stimulated by a girl's society, and when he was not. All girls knew: there was a feeling when it was all flat, disappointing and forced, and there was quite a different feeling of friendliness, easiness, and confidence when it was right.

Clear shadowless light lingered late in the garden tonight, and Norah and her mother talked on after little Barbara had finished her supper and had departed, scouting about among the garden bushes with all the stealthiness, the little pouncing rushes and fearful retreats, of a baby kitten.

"Right here at Morristown, is he?" Mrs. Oliver said. "Why, how pleasant!"

"He's at the Lake House this week with his cousins."

"And when do you see him again, dear?"

Norah smiled in the kindly dusk. For the first time in her acquaintance with him she had not felt the need of half-coaxing, half-reproaching David into the promise of another meeting. She did not know exactly when she would see him again, she merely knew that their meeting would positively occur—this time he would take care of that!

That night, when she went in to bed, she felt that she could have put her arms about the old house, laid her young face against its mellowed age and beauty. It was so kind to her; she loved it so! The spattered moonlight through motionless pear-tree branches, the glimmer of dim light that was the kitchen lamp, the bigness and graciousness of Foxaway, were a part of herself, an extension of her own personality, her sensibility: she breathed in them and through them.

She was actually in bed and had blown out her candle before the thought of her possible obligations to Barry came to disturb the dream of David. Instantly uneasiness and misgivings seized upon her full force, and she leaped out of bed and went to her mother's door.

"Awake, Mother?"

"Yes, dear. What is it, Norah? I put out my lamp because the night is so close."

Norah, a dim shape in the gloom, sat on the foot of the bed. Moonlight streamed in and lay in silver bars and angles on the floor. But the rest of the room was in darkness.

"Mother, I forgot to tell you! David said that the paper said this morning that one of the *Ladysmith's* lifeboats had been found."

"No! Not Mr. Dunsmuir, not Dr. Sassoon?"

"No. But others, seamen. And they said—these men they picked up—that Dr. Sassoon and Barry Dunsmuir in still another boat had been with them until a few weeks before, until a storm separated them. They said their rudder—or their compass, or something, had been destroyed——"

"Well, Norah, which was it? Compass or rudder—there's a difference!"

Norah laughed apologetically.

"I know. But, at any rate, they said *something* was missing, or wrong, with the other boat, but they think—or David said they think—they think very probably they're alive and can be found. Anyway, the paper said the rescue ship was going to refit somewhere—Buenos Aires, or somewhere, and make another try."

"Well," said Mrs. Oliver, "I am very glad of anything that gives their families the slightest hope, and no one could be gladder than I to see Mr. Dunsmuir safely back. It was a crazy thing to do for a man who doesn't look strong—those eyeglasses——"

"Oh, he's strong enough, I imagine. I know Dr. Sassoon was crazy to have him."

"But what I was going to say was," the older woman pursued, "that in another way we have great reason to be thankful. While there is any hope of his return that aunt of his, Mrs. Dunsmuir, can't very well drive you out of his home. We can simply remain here: that's a *great* consideration."

"Yes, that's true, too," Norah agreed, as her mother's voice dwindled to silence. "And there are other considerations, my dear mother," she thought, "that would surprise you. All we can do," she said aloud, "is wait."

"Now that you are better known here," the mother presently said, "I can't see why you and Eve can't have a little school. Mrs. Leonard was speaking about it the other day: she says there are quite a few families scattered about here in the various towns who would like to place their small children in a good school. And Mrs. Towne asked me about her mother—her mother wants to be near her—and yet it doesn't seem to work, having her right in the house."

"We'd have to put a furnace in, Mother, and anything as radical as that I think would be silly even if we could afford it. At any minute we may have to walk out."

"Well, I was just thinking, dear, that there must be *some* way to make use of a place like this——

"Unless my Norah," her mother added significantly, after a moment's silence, "is going to fall in love with someone, and leave me as Elinor did."

"On the strength of one call from Dave Howard, Mother! I'm ashamed of you."

Mrs. Oliver laughed gently, as if she were a little ashamed of herself. Presently she said, "I declare I do feel very grateful to your Mr. Dunsmuir, poor fellow."

"Grateful?"

"Oh, yes, Norah. But for him we never would have had this experience, this wonderful summer!"

Norah sat on for a while, hugging her slim young knees, staring out at the world that was swimming in hazy wide autumn moonlight.

"Yes, that's true," she said at last.

And when presently she went back to her own bed, it was of Barry she thought, as she drifted off to sleep.

Chapter XVII

A YEAR ago, maddeningly enough, it would have been simply heaven to have David ask her to go down to the city and stay overnight as his mother's guest and go to a smart musical show. It would have thrilled Norah Oliver, of the Bronx, to the roots of her being to receive from David's aforementioned mother a charming letter asking Miss Oliver, in a dashing hand, to accept the invitation. To Norah Oliver of Foxaway it meant something a little less, unfortunately; life would not stand at glad, confident morning again, where David was concerned, at least.

But, after all, she ruminated, packing her bag for the outing, if the girl doesn't care too much, the man does. That is the way of life and love. One party to every love affair cares more than the other—it was sad, it was too bad that both couldn't be in that trembling, jealous, anxious state that turned all the world upside down. But it was true.

Last year she had been the unhappy, the uncertain one. Now it almost seemed as if she and David had changed parts. She liked him, oh, she liked him immensely—he was the same handsome, careless, amusing boy he had always been, generous with his money; sure of himself; magnificent in evening dress.

But—well, there was Foxaway, now. Ridiculous as it sounded, Foxaway was tremendously important. Norah had hated her life in the city; she loved every minute of it here on the farm. She loved the crisp, cooling mornings of autumn, the thinned air and the glowing leaves; she loved breakfast warmth and comfort in the big kitchen, and the chill of the rooms where she and Barbara made beds after breakfast. She loved her books, her old square piano, her chickens, her garden; she loved the warm, grainy smell of the barns; the cows and the old horse. The days were too short for her; she grudged these lost two days down in the city; she wanted to see Barbara as the Fairy Queen in the school theatricals, and walk up to the Widow Taft's prosperous place to see Uncle Rodney in the new rôle of a complacent groom.

But David took it for granted that she was as enthusiastic over the plan as he was. He and his car were waiting for her one bright morning, and Norah kissed her mother and Barbara good-bye, and they were off for the south. It was a happy trip, and it was delicious to reach the big Howard mansion, at the end of it, and be welcomed by that very unfriendly door outside of which she had wistfully lingered ten months ago. David's mother was majestically friendly, and David's father an old dear, gallant and kindly and obviously admiring of Norah. There was a handsome married sister, fretful about some "deal of poor fool Harold's," and there was an incoherent younger brother, all convulsive laughter and grim, conscious silences, and there were dinner guests. Norah liked it all, and thrilled especially to the din of the city again—had she ever been able to live in it? And was there any other place in the world as wonderful as Fifth Avenue on a clear autumn morning, with every shop glittering, and the sidewalks filled with chattering millions, and the steeples and skyscrapers vanishing against the swimming blue of a cloudless sky?

Norah bought herself a velvet dress for the theater that night, and bought a frock for Barbara, and what she called a "darling" house gown of comfortable silken folds and lines for her mother. Judge Bailey had had his own good reasons for deciding that Miss Oliver's salary must go on at least until Barry Dunsmuir was proved dead, and Norah could indulge herself a little with a clear conscience.

She and David went to someone's house for luncheon, and to a football game in the afternoon, and then she was back in the Howard house again, luxuriating in a hot bath, making herself lovely in the new velvet, with the Vandyke collar of deep embroidery setting off her country-browned skin and gray eyes, and her hair brushed damply into rings and curves against her temples.

David wasn't making love to her exactly, all this time, for which she was secretly a little grateful. But he was all happiness, all eagerness, all attention, and any girl knows how much more that represents. They loved every minute of the inexhaustible big show: its songs, its comedians, its choruses and dances, its magnificent tableaus and its shocking little "hot spots." Afterward they went to a club, and Norah saw the famous blues singer of the show at close range, and caught one sad, appealing glance from the fringed dark tearful eyes.

But none of it—no moment of pleasure, was like the moment when they began to get up into the flaming hills again, the next afternoon, and when Norah saw familiar old hooded bridges, familiar old farms propped up on bulwarks of native stone. She could not breathe deeply enough of the cool, sweet, scented air; her voice rang with new notes, she fairly bounced on the seat beside David.

"Look, David, that's the Tafts'—that's where my uncle is being spoiled within an inch of his life. She's got the finest cows of anyone round here, and she owns a building in Morristown too, and she can't do enough for him! Adores him—and he reads Wilkie Collins and Dickens to her, evenings, and tells her about Wilson and the war."

And, "Look, David, those are the espaliered trees. We're going to try them, next year. The peaches were simply marvelous, off those walls!"

"Do you like me a little?" David asked her, at her own door.

"A lot!" But she was down in the dooryard, where Barbara was dancing up and down with excitement, and Mrs. Oliver shading her eyes with a raised hand from the afternoon sun. "Oh, you're burning leaves!" Norah exclaimed. "I'm so glad. And don't they smell delicious! Oh, and Pauline—I smell it, what is it? What's cooking?"

"It's a sopporize, for your supper!" Barbara shrilled, taking bundles with all the eagerness of the child who knows that some of them at least concern her.

"We'll see you soon, David?" Mrs. Oliver said cordially.

"Saturday, surely. And I'm coming for Thanksgiving?"

"If you like," smiled the older woman. David drove away; Norah was by this time rejoicing and exclaiming in the warm kitchen, snapping strings of parcels, being kissed, recounting her adventures, all at once.

At Thanksgiving time, in November, the old farm was shut into itself. The flowers, the meals under the elm, even the blazing leaves were gone, and the hazy, dreamy, scented afternoons. The air was sharp and tingling now, and the thinned sunlight penetrated into forgotten places, from which heavy leaves had shut it all summer long; into Norah's bedroom, into the kitchen; it lay in a bright wash of light down the white-paneled old stairway.

For Thanksgiving, of course Eve was there, and Elinor and Bill too; with Barbara and David, they were seven, and between the feast and the cold were busy all day long. Bill and Elinor had driven up from the city in their shiny new car, and Elinor had in her arms the two-months-old son who immediately became the center of attraction for everybody.

Norah loved the atmosphere of the shabby old place when the cold early dusk outside had driven them all in; when the "airtights" blazed in the bedrooms and parlor, and on the dining-room hearth the stout branches of the "upper pasture oak" that had come down in a March wind burned royally all day long.

"We can keep warm, yes!" Bill Gunther said, panting, "but ye gods, to break your leg in this weather would be to freeze to death!"

He had brought the baby in his basket down to the dining room, where Barbara was arranging nuts and raisins with exquisite care, Eve and David skirmishing about in a supposed attempt to set the table, and Elinor, Norah, Pauline, and Mrs. Oliver coming and going on countless errands through the open kitchen door.

"And you love it!" Norah told him.

"Well, yes, I do. But talk about long empty days in the country!" Bill protested. "Why, it's all you can do to get through."

Norah, flashing about everywhere, saw nothing that was not heartening and homely and dear. Through the open door she could glimpse the stately dim old parlor, with its books and square piano, its winter berries and branches of fresh dark huckleberry. The dining room was full of joyous bustle; lamps had been lighted here, there were chrysanthemums on the table, and the fire was burning steadily. The window shades had been drawn against a bleak winter dusk, but inside everything was warmth and cheer and light.

Norah's hands had been cut by wires and ropes and the stiff branches of winter shrubs. Also they were strongly scented with onion, sage, kerosene, and furniture polish. Her back was on fire; every bone in her body ached, and she knew from the present state of her feelings that she would go to sleep immediately after dinner: there was no help for it, when one got tired, hungry, cold, and then was suddenly warm, comfortable, much fed, the result was a sleep like a stupor, or a stupor called sleep.

"Barbara," she said, "stop pooring that baby! He's nice and quiet, and you'll get him crying."

"He loves me to poor him!" Barbara protested, reluctantly removing her soft little dirty smoothing hands from the baby.

"It's time to get clean for dinner anyway, darling. Come along here."

"I can dish up any time you say, now," Pauline observed, as they went through the kitchen to the washroom beyond.

"What's this heating—dish water?"

"That's dish water there in that pail."

Norah dipped the end of a towel into it forthwith, drew Barbara into the ice-cold washroom, wiped the small face with the hot towel. Barbara's roseleaf skin emerged fresh and soft from the operation, but she shuddered in the atmosphere of the washroom.

"It's freezing!"

"It's only a moment." The soap smelled cold and strong; the towel with which Norah wiped Barbara's limp little hands dry was stiff and cold too. Norah brushed the fluffy hair; took one look at her own hair and hands. "Dinner!" she said encouragingly.

Dinner was to have been at five, for there had

been no lunch today; the hands of the clock now stood at seven, and everyone was ravenous.

They found their places: Norah at one end of the table, her mother at the other, Bill, Elinor, David, Eve, Barbara placed in between, and the smoking soup ready in the old-fashioned tureen. Norah had just lifted the ladle to serve when there was a knock at the kitchen entry door.

A loud knock; they all heard it, and they looked surprise at one another. On this dark winter night, with the wind rising, who could be at the door?

The door opened: a figure, big and overcoated, was there; the man was blinking in the light.

Mrs. Oliver gave a cry of incredulous joy and ran forward, was in his arms. It was Keith, come home from Central America to see his mother, to see them all. They had not seen him for almost a year.

Chapter XVIII

Two clouds darkened the rapture of this Thanksgiving night for Norah before she could go wearily to bed.

One was Eve's odd behavior. Eve had disappeared from the family group early; dishes were hardly done and the family had gathered about the dining-room fireplace when Eve had said somewhat coldly that she had a headache; she was going to bed.

Norah, flying to the colder regions upstairs for dry things for the baby half an hour later, had found her instead standing by the window in the hall, looking out into a night in which absolutely nothing except the dim reflection of the hall itself was visible. Norah had put a quick arm about her.

"Eve, what is it? They're all downstairs playing games and having fun. What is it, dear?"

"I wish I was dead!" Eve had muttered, in a voice swollen with tears.

"Eve!"

"And I hate you!" Eve had whispered fiercely, on a sob. "You think you're so—so smart! You think you're—so wonderful. They all do! I wish I was dead!"

Norah had stood perfectly still; dazed. What on *earth*——

"David, you mean?" she had asked, in sudden understanding.

Eve had made no answer. She had turned her shoulder toward Norah and was looking at the black windowpanes again.

"I can't help that, can I?" Norah had asked, in a troubled, hurt tone.

Still there had been no answer, and after a moment Norah had gone downstairs. The happy evening had been shadowed for her from that moment, and even when Keith went upstairs and brought back Eve, a little pale but very pretty in fresh powder and lip-red, with newly-combed hair, to the circle, Norah still felt shocked and subdued. Eve sat on a hassock at her mother's feet; her linked elbows crooked against her mother's knee to support her head. She did not speak to David or glance at him; she was gentle, sympathetic, silent, not a bit like Eve.

The evening's second bad moment came half an hour later, when David had to start on the run back to Morristown. Norah wrapped herself in a heavy coat and went with him to the side door, saw that he had his coat and cap and muffler, and was laughing over sleepy goodnights when he suddenly drew her into the empty kitchen.

One dim lamp was lighted here; Pauline, ably if somewhat confusedly seconded by almost every person in the group, had long ago finished the last dish, had wiped the sink boards, and put the morning oatmeal to simmer far back on the range. The fire's eye was red through the stove coal box; the air in the kitchen was warm, and scented still by the wreck of the great turkey that Norah and Barbara had been treacherously fattening for many weeks in one of the chicken-yard pens.

"Norah!" David said. She was jumbled against him, laughing, his two big arms holding her lightly.

"Sh-h-h!" she warned him, with a glance toward the dining-room's half-opened door across the entry.

"Norah, I want you—I want you *terribly*—to marry me!" David said.

"Oh, David, how can you talk so! You're still in college, you don't even know what you're going to *be* yet."

"That doesn't matter!" David said in a low voice, holding her tightly to him.

"But it does!" She was laughing nervously, trying to free herself.

"Listen," he murmured. "I'm crazy about you!"

"Oh, please——" Norah stammered.

"You keep putting me off!" he said.

"I don't keep putting you off at all." She was actually holding him at a distance as she spoke; her hands braced in the hands that would have drawn her nearer. "Only—only we mustn't talk like this!" she said breathlessly.

"Why not?"

"Because we mustn't!"

"Norah——" His strong arms were about her again. "You can't play with me!"

"I'm not playing with you!"

"You've known all along how I felt."

"I don't think I have. I—I—anyway," Norah jerked her head in the direction of the dining room, "anyway—I couldn't—I've my mother to think of—and Eve——"

"There!" David said. His kiss against her mouth had obliterated the last words. Norah laughed breathlessly, losing her bearings for one heady minute of happiness and excitement.

"Did you like it?" he said.

"Oh, please!" she whispered. "They'll hear!"

She was sitting against the table edge; she held him off with both palms pressed against his shoulders.

"I'm mad about you!" David said.

Her head was tipped back again, his hard jaw against her jaw. Norah caught at her breath.

"Your mother——" she protested.

"Mother doesn't matter! Anyway, she thinks you're swell!"

"Mine," she added. "Mine does matter!"

"Your brother's here now. Norah, let go all the responsibilities. You've had them too long! Just—love me. Just have fun."

He was sitting beside her on the table now; the girl was turned about so that she half faced him; his big arm was about her. Norah framed his face in her two soft hands.

"David," she said thoughtfully.

"Norah."

"It's going to be—us, is it?"

"You darling," he murmured.

"I think I always thought it would be this way," Norah said.

"I know I always did. Norah, I'm so happy!"

"Yes," she agreed. "And I'm happy, too."

"As far as Mother goes——"

"Oh, let's not think of your mother. You know she won't like your marrying anyone!"

"She'll give you a tea."

"And I'll die of shyness."

"Norah, let's get married soon—right away. Let's tell your brother tomorrow. He'll make some arrangement for your mother and Eve——"

"Oh, but, David, we couldn't be married for *years!*"

"Years? What nonsense! We could be married next week."

"No, we couldn't," she said slowly, in a troubled tone.

"Oh, yes, we could. As soon as my father and mother know—in a few weeks."

But Norah did not smile, and the face at which he was looking down so lovingly—it was close to his breast—was very sober.

"I really couldn't," she said. "There's something—there's my job, you know. This place—Barbara——"

"If Dunsmuir's dead you can't go on here."

"But he may not be dead." Her senses had had their ecstatic moment; common sense was wide awake now. She disengaged herself from David's arm.

"What's the matter?" the boy asked disappointedly.

"The matter? Nothing." But her voice gave the words the lie. "I promised Mr. Dunsmuir——" she began, and stopped.

"Dunsmuir? What's *he* got to do with it, *now?*"

"Well, he sent us up here, after all."

"Yes, but that was when he expected to come back right away. You—how well did you know him, Norah? How old is he?"

There was a silence while they stood staring at each other; Norah's restraining hands still on the man's shoulders, his own locked lightly about her waist.

"Norah, you and he aren't in love with each other?"

"No," she answered, on an odd breathless note.

"Engaged?"

She hesitated. "No, of course not!" she said.

"Wasn't he engaged to some girl that's been all over the papers about it?"

"Miss Swann. Lucille Swann—yes."

"Well, then——"

"Still, I'll feel bound here until he comes back."

"But suppose he doesn't come back? Who's this old woman that's snooping round trying to get possession of the place?"

Norah laughed.

"His aunt, Mrs. Dunsmuir. She says it was left to her daughter."

"And when'll that be decided?"

"I don't know."

"But, listen, Norah," David said, sitting beside her on the table now, with one arm bracingly about her, "you don't have to hurry, darling. Here's what I want to do: I want to graduate, see?—and then have a long talk with Pop, see?—and find out what he'll do for us, see? He told me last year that he wished to goodness I would marry some nice girl, and my mother and Sidney are going abroad for a year, as soon as Sidney graduates, anyway. You close up here, get your mother and sister settled——"

"But where? Over on the Island?"

"No, not over on the Island. Eve'll get a job, won't she? And your brother will help, and the Gunthers will help—and, gosh, we'll help too. If you'd like, Norah, they could live with us—honestly!"

"Ah, you're nice!" she said affectionately, touched.

"You've carried the whole thing long enough," he went on, warming. "Please—please be nice to me, *please,* Norah."

"Norah—oh, you're in here!" Eve said, coming in. "Mother thought you were outside and that you'd catch cold!"

Norah and David were standing some feet away from each other before the sentence was finished; the three young persons looked embarrassedly at each other in the dim kitchen light.

"No—we were talking," Norah explained confusedly.

"I'm sorry," Eve said, in a hard voice. "Mother said——"

"Yes, I've got to go!" David muttered in the pause, with exultation in his brief laugh.

Norah shut the entry door behind him, shutting out also the blown windy night and the wheeling stars. She turned then to speak to Eve. But Eve was gone.

Eve and David: the troubled thought of them, and a hundred other thoughts, tossed in her heart and mind as soon as she was in bed that Thanksgiving night. She had been carried off her feet by David's insistence, his kisses. They were engaged.

But somehow it didn't feel like being engaged. There were too many considerations other than the mere excitement of loving a man, pledging herself to him.

"Why couldn't this have happened last year! I would have been in seventh heaven last year!

"But now there's Barry to think about," Norah fretted, wide awake and restless again in the lonely dark. "It would be too dangerous to marry a man with another man apt to turn up any minute. And if the papers once find out about my marrying Barry, then what a fool I'll feel announcing my engagement to David.

"I wish I could tell Mother. But it seems too preposterous to wait until now to tell her.

"Everyone will think I was Barry's mistress or something. I can't put an advertisement in the papers to say that we only saw each other seven times."

An advertisement in the papers: that had started this whole merry-go-round only a year ago.

David had said he would come over to Foxaway again on Sunday; they could talk then.

Perhaps the whole idea would seem less terrifying then. His family would probably be cool to her; well, that couldn't be helped. They were rich; his mother would have liked David to make a better marriage. But his father was a dear!

"They'll give me a tea—ugh!" Norah thought. She wondered what sort of clothes a prospective daughter-in-law must wear to a tea. "I can't afford to buy pretty things, with Mother and Eve and everything upset!" her mind fretted on.

"It's ridiculous to think of such things when you're trying to get to sleep. Everything will seem perfectly simple and easy in the morning, and after all—I'm engaged—and to David, and I've never loved anyone else.

"I'm lucky. I've everything to be thankful for, and I ought to get to sleep."

But still she felt burdened and nervous, and she could not get to sleep. She must tell David about Barry, of course; perhaps no one else need know, except old Judge Bailey, who knew already.

For the Dunsmuirs would have Foxaway: it had been so specified in Barry's will, written more than a year ago. And since Norah wouldn't ever be Barry's wife, and mightn't even be legally Barry's widow, she had no possible claim on the old place.

WIFE FOR SALE 221

"And since I can't have Foxaway," she mused, "and since David and I will have to live in the city anyway, I might as well make a new start."

She raised herself on her elbow, shook her pillow, and retreated again into the warmth and comfort of the blankets.

Foxaway: that was the rub. She loved every silvered shingle of the farm, the tree shadows against the old house, the mellow shadowy greenness of the summer garden, the spring chill, the earthy sweetness, and the rushing of freed waters in March. She loved the old books, the firelight dancing on distempered walls and shabby pewter candlesticks in the dining room, the sunshine that battered against her eastern window shutters on hot June mornings.

This was home for them all, Mother and Eve, and little Barbara and Elinor and Bill and little Bill, and now for Keith. But for Norah it was more than home: her soul had somehow grown, under the sloped old roof of Foxaway, under the mighty trees that towered above the roof. A thousand times she had said to herself that she had "come alive" there, had felt her own budding powers and possibilities expanding there.

To be sure, her first summer had had its humiliations and failures. Norah had kept the whole family in a gale of laughter this very Thanksgiving night at the dinner table, with an account of her various ventures and disappointments. She had made merry over the tavern guests who had failed to come on Sundays when chicken and ice cream had been laboriously prepared for them, and had appeared only on the occasion when she could not possibly give them a meal; the boarding home for rich children, "during their parents' absence in Europe," which had netted but one small half-pay girl during the whole season; the jam that had sugared; the four dogs Norah had accommodated for two weeks at one dollar a week, only to find herself faced with a possible damage suit for three hundred dollars for a taxi-driver's bitten hand; the hopeful little signs displayed at the Lake Hotel: "Fresh Garden Flowers for Occasions—Mending Done—Children Tutored —Honey—Cakes for Birthdays," that had attracted no notice whatsoever.

And yet, through these events themselves, and through her account of them, she had somehow lost faith neither in herself nor in Foxaway. The living *was* there; the rich and busy livelihood that would entitle her to all the joys of the chatelaine in orchard and spring house, kitchen, library, attic, cow barn and chicken runs, corn patch and elm trees and old-fashioned garden. It was merely that she had not mastered its secret as yet. That would come.

Or at least that might have come. But it was too

late now. Barry was dead, and she must take whatever steps the Howards thought wise about annulling her marriage, if it could be annulled. That would be the dignified thing to do, if she were to announce her engagement immediately.

Barry. Was he really dead? Snug in her warm bed, she thought of the eternal snows of the far, frozen South. One man, with his infinitesimal trappings of furs and tents, would be only a speck there; of no more account than a dead seal or a wind-killed gull. Was Barry lying out there, alone, and very still, his dead face turned up to the continually falling snow?

Or had the lifeboat gone down, as the ship herself had, into a cold rough heaviness of antarctic waters, dragging with it and smothering with complete indifference the tiny struggling atoms that were living, thinking, sentient men?

"He'll never see Foxaway again, and after a few weeks I won't," Norah thought. "Funny—when he said he loved it so, and I love it so. Some day I'll have a country place again, as old as this—as much like this as I can find. There must be lots of them—but of course they won't be Foxaway!

"And David," she concluded, more than halfway asleep now, and sinking into the drowsiness and comfort and dreaminess that meant sleep, "David is a darling! Engagements are probably always like this: they seem sort of confusing, sort of nervous, at first. I'll love my little apartment in New York, like Elinor's; I'll love having Mother and Eve come over for dinner; it won't take me long to forget a place I never had seen a year ago!"

She was all but off; in a half dream it seemed to her that Barry had come back—was coming to her wedding to David—her heart thumped——

Norah started up, wide awake. Barry was alive somewhere, and she was his wife—they had made that bargain——

She settled down again. This was ridiculous. She must be overtired; she *must* get to sleep.

In her mind she began resolutely to rearrange the parlor; everything must be moved. The piano—the books—the round-backed tavern chairs . . .

Norah had found a faded, distempered old photograph of the room as it had been twenty-five years ago; she had long had it in mind to restore it to its old aspect . . .

Piano here, chairs here, table here . . .

She was asleep.

Chapter XIX

KEITH'S Anne had suddenly married Fred Wilson, and Keith, while not heartbroken, was hurt in his pride and had done with girls forever. He told Norah so, when he came up for a cold snowy Christmas, and when they stoked fires and tramped white roads together.

Anne's faithlessness had perhaps opened his eyes to Norah's own stubborn loyalty; the brother and sister felt that they had never really known each other before. Norah bloomed under Keith's affection, Keith's admiration, and Keith was quite frankly captivated by this new, brown, capable, farm-keeping sister, with her uncanny knowledge of fires, draughts, eggs, fowls, fruit markets, and the whims of cattle.

He had wanted her to go back with him to Guatemala, and his mother to make her home with them both. They'd love it, Keith predicted; it was all different. Lazy, easy, white-clad, with servants obtainable for what tips alone would be in a New York apartment, and a job for Norah waiting in his company.

But now, puzzlingly enough, Elinor wanted Mother, too, for a great part of the time. The objectionable Bill had to be on the road for periods of weeks, and Elinor and her baby would be alone in the new house in Scarsdale. Elinor, despite her conduct, adored her mother; she was violently opposed to the Guatemala scheme. And to completely confuse all plans, Eve had begun, in a haughty sort of way, to quote one "Johnnie Driscoll" on all occasions. Scornfully, almost contemptuously; still, she did quote him. Young Dr. Driscoll was associated with the Olivers' family doctor, in imposing offices on Lexington Avenue; he was short, and red-headed, and given to innocent British puns, and marrying him would make Eve a subject of George the Fifth, but still——

"As for my going," Norah explained to her brother, on a cold March walk, "it wouldn't be possible. I belong here, and you and the others can come back here as often as you like."

"And what are you going to use for money and food?"

"I'll have money."

"You mean you'll marry David?"

"I mean that next month, April, I'll have to face the music. You see, David wants to announce it in May—our engagement, I mean, and to be married immediately. And before that I'll have to get a Court decision, or something."

"About back salary?"

"No, not that. That was always paid, but I was so stupid that I never found out until I saw

Judge Bailey, in September. Barry, of course, had the checks sent to the Bronx bank where he had started my account, and I had closed that out when we moved, and never thought of writing there. No, it's this, Keith," Norah went on hesitatingly. "I'll have to have our—our marriage annulled."

"Your *what?*"

She laughed nervously.

"I was married to Barry Dunsmuir, Keith."

Keith stopped short on the cold, frozen road; looked at her.

"Hit your telephone!" he said.

Norah laughed again, more naturally.

"No, really. That's what's made it all so queer. That's what made me so nervous—so half-hearted, in the very beginning. Don't you remember that I didn't want to take this job, I was all upset about it?"

"I do remember that. But you and Dunsmuir —but were you in love with each other?"

"Not exactly. But it was any port in a storm, for me."

"And he. Was he so keen to get a wife?"

"Well. In a way. He's queer, you know."

They went on walking.

"So I thought, until that's all straightened out, I'd stay here, with Mother. I couldn't marry David while there was any chance that Barry might come back."

"There isn't any chance now."

"So they all say. But if the newspapers should get all this, then how could I come smugly out with my engagement to David?"

"Mother know about you and Dunsmuir?"

"No, but I'm going to tell her. These Dunsmuirs, these cousins of Barry's, are making trouble, too," Norah went on resignedly. "Judge Bailey says we must tell them, of course. But it won't make any difference as far as Foxaway is concerned, for he left that to Hazel Dunsmuir, in his will. He left her the place, and left his money to a fund for antarctic research—fungus research, or something. Hazel thinks that she's been left money, too, I know, but Judge Bailey told me they're going to read the will next month, by court order—then my claim will come in, what they call the statutory claim of the relict—I'm the 'relict,' don't you love that?

"But just the same," she presently resumed, after her brother had given her a hand over a muddy ditch, and when they were on the descent above Foxaway, "just the same, I hate all the fuss! I hate questions, and people looking at me. And I'm afraid Mother'll be wild. She feels badly enough, going away. I wish May was over!"

"Wait a minute, Norah. You're happy over your engagement to Howard?" Keith said, catching at her arm.

"Oh, yes," Norah answered, after a second's imperceptible hesitation. "I think David will hate all this," she added, irresolutely.

"The marriage stuff?"

"Well, and the fact that I kept it all from him. And then this Lucille Swann business."

"I'd forgotten that. How about that? How do you account for it?"

"I account for it by suspecting that she's one of those pathologic cases that always announces engagements to lost men."

"I see!" As they turned in at the upper pasture gate, above the pool, Keith laughed. "It is a mess!" he conceded.

"Five weeks to May Day!" Norah said ruefully, at the kitchen door.

They were the loveliest weeks of all the year; the weeks that brought back peepers and green willow shoots, running brooks and blue skies, and the first hints of grass and lilacs. Norah watched them pass with a heavy heart.

She dreaded May Day. It was to be the beginning of so much that was new and strange, and the ending of so much that was familiar and loved. She was to tell her family, and he his family, of her engagement to David on May Day, and of their plan to be married a few weeks later. And she was to turn over Foxaway to the Dunsmuirs on that same day.

The Dunsmuirs were coming up to the Lake

House at Cattahunk, and old Judge Bailey was to drive up from Morristown, and the whole formal business of relinquishing the place that had been home to the Olivers for sixteen eventful months would take place.

Barry's will had been filed after the unsuccessful return of the second relief expedition: it gave Foxaway to Hazel Dunsmuir. That was flat. Barry was officially dead, as Dr. Sassoon was dead. The great explorer's body had been found buried deep in an iceberg that was frozen tight to the ice-foot off Ross Sea. His journal, wrapped safely in the collapsed tent, had ended the story: *"No food since Friday; we think this is Monday, September third,"* said the penciled lines. *"We are drifting toward land; Jens did not get the seal. Bad, bad, bad. Barry——"*

That was all, and even that bit was blurred and illegible. Norah had pored over the meager newspaper reports hungrily; there was no more. It was all over.

And immediately she had had letters from Mrs. Dunsmuir and Judge Bailey. They would be up as soon as the rains ended; would she be ready to surrender the farm?

Yes, of course she would. She had no choice. Norah's heart had ached fiercely at the necessity; she had consoled herself with the thought that, after all, she and David could not live there after they were married, and the expense of keeping so large a place going would be out of the question for them, anyway. Indeed, finances were already worrisome: her mother's plans, Eve's plans, her own clothes for engagement parties, would all cost money, and money was scarce.

"You could get something, you know, from Dunsmuir's estate," Keith hopefully observed one night when they were talking.

"I don't want to! I'd take Foxaway fast enough, if I could get it. But I'm not his wife, Keith, nor his widow, and I couldn't put in any claim. I only want enough to get clear and away!"

"If it was only a thousand," Keith said, "it would help clearing up here and getting Mother settled in town."

"A thousand!" It sounded to her like an immense sum.

"Does the Howard family know about your marrying him?"

"No." The subject made her nervous. "And I don't want them to," she said. "I'm going to tell David, but not his father and mother; it sounds so silly. It sounds so common! I just want to forget it."

"Well, I think you're rather a fool not to take what you can get," Keith observed mildly. He had been transferred, in midwinter, from his company's Guatemala office to their New York office; he was shortly to go back to Central America, and hoped this time to take his mother with him. Eve, taking a correspondence course in interior decoration, was also at home; the Olivers had enjoyed a brief country interval freed from the city's strain and pressure; now it appeared that Foxaway had been only a reprieve, not a cure for their troubles. From the time of their father's death they had all been drifters, taking the line of least resistance, formulating no plans; flotsam on the tremendous current of the biggest city's turbulent waters.

Just this last year Norah had hoped for something better: background, occupation, significance in her life. It had been defeated; this first day of May was to see everything changed. And dearly as she loved David—and she told herself continually that no girl could have a more splendid fate than to marry David—she knew that she would surrender Foxaway with a sense of bafflement, of defeat.

David would take care of her now. But at Foxaway she would have been able to take care of herself.

Keith had a few hundreds; Norah less than a hundred dollars; David assured her enthusiastically that his father would lend the Olivers any amount. They would get through, of course; they would be quietly married, everything would straighten out. But there was no sense of triumph, of excitement about it. Once again it was rather like turning into a port in a storm, not caring much what the port might be.

"If only I were sure I loved David!" she would say, half aloud, as she scraped the old wooden bowl of scraps for the chickens, or wandered up the lane to call Barbara and her school gang for a Saturday lunch. And she would answer herself at once: "Of course you do! Isn't this what you've been praying for?"

At all events, David was in no doubt of it. He was a completely normal person, which meant, at twenty-five, that he thought well of rich, handsome, popular David Howard. Norah never saw a sign of uncertainty as to his plans or hers, in David.

And under all these plans, for her, burned the wretchedness, the jealousy that stirred in her whenever she thought of turning Foxaway over to the Dunsmuirs—those complacent, proud, cold cousins who would take the place she loved and ruin it, chop down trees and destroy the old barns and fences, throw out the daguerreotypes and the samplers, send up sets of new china and modern chairs and beds.

Norah, a few days before the change, packed away in a special trunk of her own some certain books and letters and old dim photographs. After all, it wasn't quite stealing; after all, she had some right to Barry's old letters and his little-boy diary, written with a bursting heart in his first boarding school.

Norah's eyes had been wet more than once, as she read the old record, and she had seen through a blur of tears the picture of the little boy in his sailor suit, leaning against his seated mother's knee, looking up with infinite content and adoration into the tenderness and love in her face. Not a strong-looking little boy, not handsome, but it was a good, wistful, hopeful little face. And shortly after the old photograph had been taken, she knew, that mother had been gone, and the ten-year-old Barry had been packed off to a Western school that had meant only torture and loneliness to his odd little spirit; Norah knew this, because she had read his tear-grimed, muddied, inky letters to his dead mother—letters jealously shut away into his private notebooks, but presently to be stored here, in the old attic, among his arithmetics and grammars, and all the miscellany that had been sent home after him, when he had been invalided back to the farm, a few years later.

"I am writing to you, Mother, if even you're dead," one of them, written weeks after the little boy in black had stood crying at her grave, explained seriously, *"because so far I haven't any other friends."*

"They laugh at me when I read, and a bunch of them come round me every night, and say I'm

yellow," another letter said. *"And these are the little kids from the seventh, and I cannot lick them or they would yell. It is only one hundred and seven days to vacation but it seems quite a while."*

"I went out into the woods tonight, and prayed that you or someone would make my father take me out of here," one broken-hearted document confessed. *"They think I am no good and I guess I am no good."*

The little-boy earnestness, the confused terms and words, had captivated Norah, reading her eyes blind on a hot, rainy afternoon, up in the queer scents and shadows of the attic.

"If even you're dead," and *"Thirsday, your burthday,"* *"hooping couhg,"* and *"your boy that you love, Buddy."* What a tragedy the going of one gentle woman could be to a little boy's heart! And sometimes Norah found herself laughing, with wet eyes, when the painstaking pen had toiled on the schoolboy phrases: *"and lissen what do you think,"* or *"and looky, Mother, here's what."*

Foxaway ran all through the letters. Evidently the homesick little fellow had adored the farm. The bridge, the pool, the trees he had climbed, the roofs upon which he had torn his small garments, the windmill and the barns, were his paradise. *"Gee, if I and you could live there, like we were last Easter, and you could make me pan-*

cakes, and we could fire the B. B.!" little Barry had written longingly. *"Don't let Uncle sell Foxaway unless he wants to break us kids heartss!"*

It had been written more than twenty years ago, but she knew just how the writer had felt. It *was* heartbreaking, to have to leave Foxaway, when one once had known it—when one loved it. Into every hour that she spent there, into every scent and sound and sight, there began to be, for Norah, the ache of the passing. She could not hold it; she must presently say good-bye to it, and forever.

Even if she didn't marry David right away— but of course she was going to marry David right away. . . .

Even if she didn't marry David right away— even if she didn't marry David. . . .

The phrase came to her on the last sweet lingering day of April, twenty-four hours before the time appointed to tell her people and his people, and the world, that she meant to marry David next month. Norah tried to put it out of her heart.

But there was a spring in it, a lift in it, just the same. It seemed to take a great weight off her heart even to say it. Nobody could force her to marry David right now. A few months' delay —a year's delay . . .

She could plead that considering the strange

circumstances of her first marriage she wanted more time in which to prepare for her second. Or she could just say she didn't want to marry anybody right now.

Norah discovered that she really had been afraid of what David and David's family would think of her affair with Barry. She had lost many hours in worrying, many nights in anxious anticipation as to what they would say. Now, with intense relief, she realized that nobody could blame her for anything at all, if she simply and firmly declined to be engaged until all these other matters were settled.

Then what would she do this summer? Well, that didn't matter. She was no cripple, and with Keith, Eve, and Mother all more or less settled, she felt she could do anything. Why, it would be simpler—it would be great fun, to go home with Pauline, to her inexhaustibly entertaining family, and look about from there for possible fields of work. "I don't *have* to marry anyone!" Norah gasped in her soul.

Chapter XX

THE thought of being free for a little while was intoxicating—yes, free even from the niceness and the affection of David! Life had too often forced Norah to please other persons; she had been pleasing Mother and Eve and Keith all her life long. Now she wouldn't have to please anyone; let them think what they liked of her, let them be amazed at her first marriage, and scandalized at her indefinite postponement of her second, let them turn her out of Foxaway —she would be free!

"It would only mean beginning to try to please David," she thought, "and his mother and father, and having awful dinners with his sister. I won't do it!"

"Won't do what?" Eve asked in her sulky, sweet voice, on a certain wet stormy afternoon, when the sisters were sharing a sitting-room fire. Norah realized that she had been talking aloud to herself.

"Oh, nothing!" she answered, with a guilty little laugh.

"No, but what?" Eve pursued.

"Nothing, really. I suppose," Norah went on honestly, "I was thinking of David."

"I know you were!" Eve answered quickly. "You're going to tell the Howards tomorrow night, aren't you?"

"Well, soon, I suppose." Norah felt the trap closing about her again.

"But aren't you going down with David tomorrow?" the younger sister pursued relentlessly.

"He said something about it. Tomorrow or next day."

"Then it'll be in the paper," Eve said in a suffocated voice.

Norah looked up from the cuffs and collar she was basting into a dark blue silk gown.

"Eve——" she said, and stopped.

Eve, manicuring her pretty hands carefully, kept her lashes down. But as Norah said nothing more, but continued to regard her with concern, she suddenly shrugged, laughed, and looked up.

"Well, you knew it!" she observed coldly.

"I suspected it, Thanksgiving night," Norah returned slowly. "But I hadn't thought of it, since."

"Don't think of it now!" Eve said flippantly.

"Don't you like Dr. Driscoll?" Norah asked.

"Johnnie Driscoll!" Eve exclaimed, angry tears in her eyes.

"Well, he likes you," Norah observed rather lamely.

"And David likes you," Eve finished it dryly.

"I've always liked David," the older sister asserted, as if speaking to herself.

"You did!" Eve said bitterly. "You don't now. You were crazy about him before we came up here! You don't even like him now—not as I do! I'm not ashamed of it—I told him!"

"You did not tell him!"

"I did, a week ago. I cried—we were up by the spring, getting cress, and I hurt my hand on a slipping rock, when we climbed up back of the pool, and he kissed me!" Eve stated, childishly triumphant.

"He kissed you as my little sister," Norah said, ashamed for Eve.

"I know he did, he said he did!" Eve conceded fiercely. "I'm not trying to get him away from you, I'm just sick—I'm *sick*. You get everything, and I get nothing! You'll marry him, and you'll have him, and he'll never know how I could have——"

"Oh, *please!*" Norah interrupted.

"You are going to marry him, aren't you, Norah?" Eve asked, after a long pause, forlorn hope in her voice.

"We're—you know that—we're announcing it right away," Norah reminded her, in a slow, troubled voice. "But what I was thinking," she went on, "was that I'd like not to have it so soon. David doesn't know about me and Barry Dunsmuir, yet—his mother and father will make a fuss; the newspapers may get it. I was thinking, today, that I'd like to put it off a little while, announcing it. And if you felt—I mean, since you feel——"

She hesitated, and Eve, suddenly ashen white, twisted about in her chair and leaned over so that her face was very close to her sister's face.

"Now, listen, Norah," she said, on a swift threatening whisper, "you put off your engagement with David on my account, tomorrow, and I'll kill myself! I will, I tell you! You go through with this, and be engaged, and be married, and have it over, or I'll get out! It's bad enough for me as it is, I'm *sick* with it—I'm *crazy* with it, but I'll not have you being heroic and sisterly and self-sacrificing——"

"Shut up, Eve!" Norah interrupted sharply. "Don't talk like a fool!"

"I'm not talking like a fool," Eve protested, but in a milder tone. "It's true, and I'll prove it, if you throw David Howard down. In the first place, he can't stand me, and if he was free for twenty years I'd never take him—I have *some* pride! And more than that, you used to be crazy about him, and we all knew it, and if you hadn't been mulled up here in this God-forsaken place, brooding over old letters and all but wearing hoopskirts and ringlets——"

"What!" Norah gasped, too much amazed to retain her anger.

"Well, you've forgotten what the city's like!" Eve rushed on. "You've forgotten that it's smart to go to shows, and dress like a human being, and read something later than Trollope, and get your eggs out of boxes, like a Christian, instead of scrambling around under hot feathery hens——"

Norah's delicious laugh rang out gayly; honest surprise was mingled with amusement in her voice when she exclaimed:

"Oh, Eve, I'm not as bad as all that!"

"You *are*," Eve insisted firmly, pleased with the effect she had made. "And part of all this silliness about banjo clocks and tintypes and applewood highboys is because you got a crush on that squinty little *gnome*—" Eve had searched for the last word, and she brought it out with relish, "that squinty little gnome Barry Dunsmuir!" she finished.

The laughter died out of Norah's face, and she said quickly, her cheeks reddening: "I did not!"

"You did, too!"

"He was different from anyone I ever knew —he was a *man,* anyway," Norah conceded reluctantly, surprised herself to realize that there was something here, as Eve had so crudely indicated, that she had not quite admitted to herself. "But since he's dead, and since we have to leave

Foxaway," she added suddenly cooling, "it doesn't matter, does it?"

"It matters if it's going to make you treat David badly, think that you can play fast and loose with your whole life's happiness!" Eve answered severely.

"Of course I'm not going to treat David badly —of course I'm not going to ruin my life by any such nonsense as that! After all, I'm twenty-five," Norah said proudly, and for a while neither spoke again. Tomorrow would be May first, Norah reflected, the day when all the changes would begin. It was too late to begin to have misgivings, scruples, now.

The dawn came with heavenly softness and warmth, after days of rain. Ending the winter's long white truce, and the slow wet advance of the reluctant spring, this singing morning showed Foxaway at its lovely best. Their forces gathered under cover, leaves and grass and fruit blossoms were suddenly in their fragrant and glorious beginnings. Shadows on the north side of the farm buildings were still wet and frosty, and there was a chill in the morning air, but by ten o'clock the washed gold and green world sparkled in hot sunshine; birds looped the garden shrubs, bursting their throats with song.

The plum tree, a great popcorn ball of white, buzzed with bees; up the grassy slope Norah could see the rich blue of the sky with the snowy blossoms bunched against it; her heart ached—ached.

The Dunsmuirs were due at eleven; they came early. Judge Bailey was not yet there. Norah sat with her guests on the grass under the great elm trees that were opening new wet leaves; Keith had moved some shabby chairs out here, and the sun filtered down pleasantly on the ladies' heads through the high branches.

"You've certainly done wonders for the old place!" Hazel Dunsmuir said, with a note of apology in her voice.

"I've not spent much money," Norah answered, with her own friendly smile. "But we've polished up some of the old things, and bought a few at country auctions—and we've had fires out here, and raked things up."

"We intend to move in next month," Hazel said. "Miss Swann is to spend the summer with us."

"We go out toward the end of the week," Norah explained.

"It was a darling thing for him to do—leave me this place," the other girl observed, with a complacent glance about.

"I hope he left you something to run it with!" her mother put in sharply.

"I was wondering if you would ever—rent Foxaway?" Norah asked.

"Rent it?" Mrs. Dunsmuir asked briskly. "Do you know of anyone who could rent it?"

Norah was absently pulling the ears of the Airedale, who stood at her knee anxiously watching her.

"No, not now," she answered slowly. Her heart was lead. "I wanted to ask you about Binge," she added, indicating the dog. "I'd be so glad to find him a good home. His owner left him here when he was only a puppy last year, and I've—we're all fond of him."

"I don't know. I know we all hate dogs," Hazel said.

"Who's the child?" Mrs. Dunsmuir asked, as Binge leaped away in little Barbara's wake.

"I've had her here, boarding. Her mother's working hard and can't have Barbara with her. When we go down to the city I'm going to try to find her some place to stay. We've all grown fond of the little thing."

"Mama, we ought to have all that stuff torn down, we don't need stables and cow houses," Hazel, not listening, said suddenly.

"There was one more thing," Norah began, stabbed as the other girl spoke by one glance at the lovely old barns and stables: "Pauline. She's been here with me since we came, and she'd be glad to stay, I know. Her people have had sickness—she's helping them. She's a wonderful worker, and nice; she's a great friend of mine."

"We're bringing our own servants," Hazel stated flatly.

"Oh, why does Foxaway have to be so lovely today!" Norah thought, as in the pause they heard the birds and bees again and the bubbling rush of water at the spring pool. Aloud she said nothing.

There was the sound of a motorcar down the road; the old Judge arrived, late and apologetic.

He drove his car almost up to the group under the elms, and getting out, flushed, hot, troubled, he introduced his companion to the Olivers: Mr. Lippincot. Keith, bringing chairs, joined them on the grass.

Mr. Lippincot was evidently the Dunsmuirs' lawyer. He carried a briefcase with him; he was a handsome, dark-eyed young fellow of perhaps thirty-five, and Norah saw Hazel immediately indicate a seat beside her own and send him a look of confidence and triumphant expectation. She was puzzled by his answering look, and she saw that Hazel was. His disturbed glance at his young client indicated that something was amiss; he sighed, shook his head, and wiped his forehead with his handkerchief.

"What is it?" Hazel, her expression instantly changing, asked alarmedly.

"Why—but wait," the lawyer answered, with a jerk of his head toward the old Judge.

Perspiring, breathless, Judge Bailey was fumbling with the clasps of his briefcase. He brought out a mass of papers.

"Mrs. Dunsmuir—Hazel," he began abruptly, "I've been trying to get you by telephone all morning. I wanted to see you before this—this meeting. I've been working all night—fact," he repeated, with a glance about the circle, "I've not had my clothes off all night!"

"But what's *happened?*" Hazel demanded sharply, anxiously. For it was obvious that something had happened.

"Most extraordinary thing I have ever known!" the old Judge answered agitatedly. "They sent poor Barry's boxes back from Hobart,—started 'em weeks ago. They arrived yesterday."

"Wouldn't those be mine?" Hazel asked quickly.

"Not until the estate is settled," her own lawyer said, in a low, warning tone.

"Oh, well," she conceded unwillingly.

"His books and papers and some clothing?" Norah asked. "He wrote me he had taken too many blankets, and he was storing his extra coat."

"Wrote you!" Hazel exclaimed, with a glance for Norah.

"Wait just a moment——" Tom Lippincot warned her again.

"He had written another will, in Hobart," Judge Bailey said.

Nobody quite grasped this, for a moment of surprise and silence; then the younger lawyer confirmed it, dryly:

"There is a will later than the one we read the other day, Miss Dunsmuir. It was signed on March eighth, in Hobart."

"Well—what of it?" Hazel asked sharply.

"It leaves—" Lippincot cleared his throat, "it leaves everything of which he died possessed to his wife," he said.

"To—*what!*" Hazel exclaimed. "He wasn't married! He was engaged to Lucille Swann, everyone knows that!"

"He didn't mention Miss Swann," Judge Bailey said.

"This is the young lady?" Tom Lippincot asked, with a glance at Norah. Norah's amazed and confused look went from one face to the other in turn; she was very white.

There was a stupefied moment of silence. Hazel Dunsmuir and her mother exchanged an outraged glance, and both laughed briefly.

Judge Bailey then said to Norah, "On the twenty-seventh of December, sixteen months ago, you were married to Barry Dunsmuir, my dear, weren't you?"

"Yes, sir," Norah whispered, her face suddenly hot. She heard Mrs. Dunsmuir gasp; she heard Hazel's incredulous sniff.

"He states in his will," the old man went on, glancing at some notes that lay before him, "that because of your affection for this place he leaves it to you, and with it every other thing of which he dies possessed."

Another silence; this time electric, sulphurous.

"Barry!" Norah stammered then, dazedly.

"He says to 'his dearly beloved wife,'" the Judge said, smiling.

"But—but not *Foxaway!*" she exclaimed.

"This is your own home now, Miss—Mrs. Dunsmuir!" the old man assured her.

"I don't believe one word of it!" Hazel protested boldly. "I never heard anything so—so silly! How dares this—this girl, who was merely his secretary—and he was engaged to Lucille, she said so!—how dares——"

"Let me talk for you," her own lawyer put in swiftly, touching her arm.

"No, I won't!" Hazel answered angrily, shaking off his hand. "That will isn't legal. I don't believe for one second it's legal! Who knows whether this story of a marriage is——"

"You may depend on me to protect your interests," Tom Lippincot reminded her in an aside. "I *beg* you——".

Judge Bailey looked at her over his glasses.

"I have authenticated the marriage," he said mildly. "I have known of it for some time."

"Then I call you nothing but a *cheat*——" Hazel was beginning hotly, when her mother stopped her.

"Sit down," said Mrs. Dunsmuir coldly, and Hazel subsided into her chair.

Norah in turn was on her feet; shining eyes on the Judge, fingers touching her cheek.

"But did you say—did you say that Barry left me Foxaway?"

"He left everything he had to his 'dearly beloved wife,'" the Judge answered, enjoying his right to tell her.

"His 'dearly beloved wife'!" Norah whispered. And, beginning to cry, she dropped down on Keith's knee and locked her arms about her brother's neck.

"This place—belongs to my sister?" Keith asked, clearing his throat.

"And a good deal more than that," Judge Bailey told him. "Barry had just come into his uncle's money, and old Dr. Dunsmuir was considerably richer than any of us thought. Even Barry probably never knew what he had—perhaps that's why he lumped it as 'everything.' There's this place, with the stock and furniture, and there's a hundred thousand in bonds—perhaps a little more. Then there is a business building in Morristown——"

"Perhaps you will inform me," Mrs. Dunsmuir's voice, cutting icily into the pause, said coldly, "exactly what evidence you have that this extraordinary story is true?"

"We have the evidence of the will, madam. And the wedding license."

This was the old Judge. The lawyer added, "The name is mentioned, Mrs. Dunsmuir." He read it from a card: "Norah Oliver Dunsmuir."

"Oh, Keith," Norah breathed, sitting up, wiping away tears, "it isn't true!"

"It is," he said.

"But I didn't think Barry had any money!"

"His uncle left him a comfortable fortune," Mr. Lippincot said. "More than perhaps he knew, when he went away. The estate was not settled then. Nobody suspected that Dr. Dunsmuir was so well-to-do!"

"Congratulations, Norah!" Keith said, kissing her.

"Upon her husband's death—certainly," Mrs. Dunsmuir added acidly.

"But, Mama," Hazel asked suspiciously, hotly, "what of Lucille? *She* was engaged to Barry—surely she has some rights—surely we all have some rights?"

"You and your mother were mentioned, Miss Dunsmuir," the Judge assured her, "a handsome legacy—ten thousand dollars apiece, I believe."

"I call that an insult! And Lucille—my dearest friend, who was going to marry Barry?" Hazel demanded angrily, imperiously.

"There was no reference to her."

"I want to congratulate you upon your secrecy, Miss Oliver," Mrs. Dunsmuir observed stingingly. "You certainly kept us all in the dark, whatever your motive was."

"I am engaged to be married to another man," Norah said with dignity. "I didn't see any use in telling everyone that I had married Mr. Dunsmuir. Foxaway was all I cared about, and you had that. I didn't know," she added with candor, "that he was so rich—he had said he wasn't rich."

"The estate was not settled when he went away," Judge Bailey repeated. "I think it was a surprise to us all that Dr. Dunsmuir had so much. Probably Barry never knew it. He was indifferent to money, poor boy!"

"Not for the money, but for various reasons connected with the family," Mrs. Dunsmuir observed, getting ready to sweep with great hauteur to her car, "it may be necessary to break that will. I don't say it will be: I say it may be. This place and dear Uncle's things are very dear to me—very dear. If I felt that it was against his wish to have strangers here, I would take every necessary step——"

"I'd like to go up to the hotel with you and discuss this," the lawyer murmured at her side. He was the only one of the trio who turned to say good-bye; the Dunsmuirs departed without that formality.

Chapter XXI

JUDGE BAILEY lingered for a few minutes, congratulating the confused and ecstatic, laughing and crying Norah, and assuring her of his readiness to help her in any way that he might with her inheritance. On a sudden impulse, her hand on his shoulder, Norah kissed him good-bye.

Then he too went away, and the immediate shouts of Norah and Keith brought everyone on the place to the scene instantly. Eve, drying her hair, came running from the upper porch, Barbara ran back with the dog at her heels, Mrs. Oliver came, amazed and fearful, from her peaceful rocker in the parlor, and Pauline rushed from the kitchen.

"It's mine, Mother—Foxaway's mine!" Norah laughed and sobbed, interrupting her wild dance on the grass with Keith. "He left it to me—and money, thousands of dollars! Mother —kiss me. I'm laughing and I don't know why I'm crying! 'To my beloved wife'—that's the way the will was! Eve, we can live here, we can have an old car——"

"Sit down, dear," Mrs. Oliver said gently. "You're all right, my darling, but you've been doing too much—working too hard."

"Mother, it's true," Keith said, eager, breathless, laughing himself. "Barry Dunsmuir left a new will, at Hobart—it's just arrived. He had a lot more money than anyone thought; and it's all for Norah, his 'beloved wife.'"

"Norah Oliver, wipe your eyes and sit down and act like a human being!" the mother said, in sharp annoyance. "What *is* all this? How could Norah possibly have married Mr. Dunsmuir?"

Norah slid on her knees on the grass beside her mother, locked her arms about her.

"Mother, I did. And he's left me Foxaway! It's mine!"

The sense of miracle was inexhaustible to them all. Barbara had to hear what the uproar meant and rejoice; Pauline and Norah kissed each other in their excitement. The farm, swimming in the hot sweetness of a May noon, rang with their voices and their laughter.

Presently David came in on their revels. Norah had been about to start, with her brother and sister, upon a hilarious tour of the place that seemed to her now sparkling with a new beauty and charm, when David's car came up the old road.

They had to tell David, and he was bewildered and amazed as the others had been. But immediately there was a slight change in Norah's mood, reflecting one she was quick to feel in his own. Her great news wasn't such great news to David.

"Now you won't want to get married right away!" he said, drawing her aside, smiling down ruefully upon her excitement and happiness. "I can't live up here: I've got a job. What about that?"

"Couldn't we live up here, David? Now that we have enough money to start a school or do anything we like?"

"My mother and father would think I was crazy. And besides, you wouldn't like it, up here in this quiet place all the year round."

"Oh, but that's just it. I *would*. And it's *mine*."

"I know, Norah, but lots of people have these old country places, and they're no good except for a few months in summer. I wanted you to come down this week," David said, very handsome and possessive in his white regalia. "Mother wanted you to stay with her; I've got her note, and she won't understand if you don't come."

Norah looked up at the house.

"I don't think I could leave Foxaway *now*—" she murmured, "and you see—there'll be a lot to fix—and there's no such hurry as there was. Judge Bailey said there would be papers—arrangements——"

"And my mother'll have to hear of Barry!" David said.

"I suppose so. Will she mind?"

He laughed, shrugged.

"I don't think so! But—you never told me, Norah!" David reproached her. "You never said you had been married."

"How could I? It was only the day he went away, poor fellow."

"But what was the big idea?"

"Oh, he had thought he would be here at Foxaway, writing his book, and he wanted me here too. And then he got this chance to go with Dr. Sassoon."

But she was hardly thinking of what she was saying. There was a light in her eyes, a glow on her face. Her look wandered to the blossoming orchard, the rise of green hillside beneath it; the height of the overhanging trees, and, turning, she included in a long glance of love and admiration the old high-hipped house with its brick chimneys, its small-paned windows, its weather-seasoned walls dappled delicately today with spring sunshine and mellow blossom shadows.

"David, imagine it mine! The books and the bookcases, and the wood pile, and the cows!"

"I know," David said slowly.

Eve and Keith came up to them, and Norah, including them in what she said, and speaking loudly enough for her mother, in her chair on the grass, to hear, exclaimed exultantly:

"Mother, we'll have electric light put in, and

pipes. We'll have the bathroom upstairs in the little hall room! I'll get old-fashioned lamp fixtures—pewter and china. And we'll have the Taft boy look for a nice second-hand car, so we can cruise about everywhere all summer!"

There was an interruption.

"First, if you please, my thousand guilders!" a high voice near by said, with a laugh through it.

Norah turned, they all turned to face the speaker. They saw a small, shabby, grinning man in somewhat rough clothing standing a dozen feet away. He had come down through the grape arbor, perhaps; no one had heard him approach.

"Barry!" Norah said in a whisper, after a stupefied silence. "Barry Dunsmuir!"

"First, if you please," he repeated, in that voice of keen mischievous relish that she had not heard for sixteen long months, "my thousand guilders!"

Chapter XXII

FOR a long minute they all stood looking at each other. Eve and Keith and their mother were merely wide-eyed, speechless, but Norah had turned very white, and David's face was red with a resentful flush.

"Barry!" Norah stammered finally. She went toward him, took his hand, turned toward the others. "He's back," she said. "I'm—I'm so glad you're back! We thought——"

"You thought I was dead!" Barry supplied, as she hesitated. "I nearly was. Norah, you didn't think you'd see me again, did you? You felt badly, I know."

Norah spoke steadily, simply.

"I was afraid you had suffered horribly—been in the water for days, or were hungry," she said. "That made me feel badly."

The expression on Barry's face changed, sobered. He spoke in a lower tone, his keen eyes fixed on Norah.

"I did suffer horribly, as you say. Let's—shall we?—sit down."

But first he went to take Mrs. Oliver's frail hand.

"You've had a dreadful experience, I'm afraid, Mr. Dunsmuir," Norah's mother said, almost timidly. For there was a dark look on his thin, keen face.

"I'll tell you about it some day," Barry said, sitting down near her chair.

He looked about appreciatively at the world of sunshine, of shadow on trembling new green, of scents and sweetness and farm sounds.

"My God, how lovely the old place is!" he said, under his breath. He glanced about the circle that was smitten to silence, and smiled his odd smile. "I've seen this often enough, in the past year!" he added. "Every leaf of it, every shingle."

Norah found her voice.

"Where do you come from now? Are you hungry? Would you let me——"

"I had breakfast of ham and eggs and grapefruit and waffles in a Pullman train, three hours ago!" Barry interrupted.

"You don't know how strange this is!" she said. "The papers—do they know you're back?"

"The papers never know anything, Norah. No," he added, in a bitter undertone, as if he were speaking to himself, "the papers don't know it. What is there for them to know? I don't amount to anything—and Sassoon's dead!"

"You've survived some experiences," Keith observed respectfully, and Norah saw Barry's keen, quick, appreciative glance move to her brother.

"Some experiences you don't want to survive!" he said briefly. Immediately he looked at Norah. "Well, you look blooming, you're as brown as an Indian!" he observed.

Her color came up as she laughed defensively. "Oh, I'm a—I'm a country woman, now!"

"Like the place, eh?" he asked shrewdly.

"Love it," Norah answered bravely.

"We—you must excuse our not in the least—expecting you, Mr. Dunsmuir," Mrs. Oliver faltered. "We only knew—the family only knew of your—your marriage to our Norah here, a few moments ago. Just this morning Judge Bailey was here, reading your—this sounds so dreadful!" Norah's mother interrupted herself to stammer apologetically, "your will—that you wrote at Hobart, more than a year ago, and your cousin, Miss Dunsmuir, was terribly upset to find out that you had been married."

Barry, his color better, and his laugh almost its old self, put in briskly:

"No! Not this morning—Hazel and Judge Bailey? Why didn't I get here an hour earlier! And they read the will, did they, Norah? And you found out that I'd left you everything, eh?"

For some reason, as he smiled triumphantly at her, Norah found her eyes full of tears. She looked away into space.

"It's all been—so surprising," Mrs. Oliver explained again hesitatingly, her own eyes watering in sympathy with Norah's emotion. "She felt so badly about leaving the farm—and then David—David," Norah's mother, who was incapable of deception or even of diplomacy of the mildest sort, proceeded candidly, "had never even heard of Norah's marriage! And he expected—they were going to tell his family——"

"Mother!" Norah interpolated, laughing, her cheeks aflame, and her eyes suddenly dried. "It is a little late for that!"

Mrs. Oliver, appearing to realize suddenly the relationship in which Norah stood to Barry, caught her breath, exclaiming, "Oh, my gracious!" and was silent.

"You see," Norah said to Barry simply, "we thought of course when Dr. Sassoon was found, and when months and months went by——"

"Why shouldn't you?" Barry asked sensibly, as she hesitated.

"We thought you were—lost, down there somewhere. The second relief expedition came back, and they found the last lifeboat, off Elephant Island. And there was no news."

"According to the courts of New York City, you're dead all right, Mr. Dunsmuir!" Keith told him, with a laugh. Norah was pleased to see Barry laugh back, quite spontaneously.

"I suppose so. Well, but here I am, alive," Barry responded alertly. "And we have to go on from here, don't we, Norah? Where do we start?"

"I thought we ought to start with food," Norah answered, with a smile. "Somehow, with antarctic explorers, food seems to be the great thing!"

"You're quite right," he said approvingly. "When you've gone back over your own trail, Mrs. Oliver, to find the place where dogs were killed, and dug up their old blood from the snow——"

"Oh, don't!" Mrs. Oliver said faintly, closing her eyes.

"Then it takes you months—*years,* to catch up on your food," Barry said. "You'll have a hard time keeping me fed, Norah."

She met the teasing challenge bravely.

"We'll do it."

"But—I was going to ask you something," Keith began, and Norah saw, with surprise, and a confused sense of something like pride, that her young brother was immensely impressed with the older man, "I was going to ask you something," Keith repeated, "but perhaps you don't want to talk about it all, yet."

"Why shouldn't I?" Barry asked. Pouncing again, even now, Norah thought. "What were you going to ask?"

"Why, where you've been, all this time, what you've been doing?" Keith recommenced.

"It was all simple enough," Barry answered, the shadow Norah had seen lighten darkening again on his sensitive thin face. "On the fourth night of the storm our ship went down—we struck a gale in the Forties, and after three days of it the *Ladysmith* went dead—no more life in her. The pumps were filled with oil and lint, and we had to draw the fires, because she'd shipped so much water in the engine room. The Chief——" His voice changed when he said the word, and he looked away for a second, losing the thread of his talk. "The Chief was everywhere," he presently went on, as if half to himself. "He made us some coffee on a primus, when the decks were listed so that you had to hook your arm through the deck rail to hang on at all. We lost two of our boats, he filled the others himself, stood there shouting at the men, name after name—he knew 'em all! Then we cut the dogs loose—I saw Kane's dog jump into one of the boats—the seas were running like mountains. Then he and I took the raft—we had to tie ourselves on. Afterward, the next day, I guess, when things were quieter, we picked up four men on the old painting planks. And a while later we dragged the raft onto a berg; she was moving southeast, against the big barrier, but she wouldn't touch. We had—there were six of us and two dogs—we had the boat raft, and her equipment, and guns. We were thirty-three days on the ice—we got one seal, and we ate the dogs——"

"Oh, no!" Norah gasped, her eyes fixed upon him, her lips parted.

"Oh, yes, Norah! We kept trying to get across the ice-foot to the mainland—we couldn't. One night the Chief said we must get the raft down, there was a lead there. We packed what we had on the raft, and when the ice began to crack, we got ready to launch her. The wind came up—it was black dark, and the ice was churning under us, big pieces were splitting off our berg, and killers were sailing up and down. I was kneeling on the raft, trying to tie some ropes, everything rocking and roaring, and pitchy dark, when the edge of the berg went down, she was split in the middle, and I on the raft, and the others on the other side. The waters went over me, I hung onto a rope, and she righted herself and went on in the pack. A boat would have been kindling wood in five minutes, the raft was rubber and barrels, roped, and she got through.

"This went on for nights—days. After a while the moon came out, and I was out of the pack, drifting on a blue ocean—no signs of the others anywhere. Everything had been washed overboard, I had nothing, I didn't know anything, and I was dead tired. I must have gone to sleep.

—After a while I waked up on a little whaler; hardly more than a big rowboat, she was. Three Danes were on board—brothers, they didn't care much about me nor ask me any questions. They thought I was lost from an exploring party of Englishmen that went in there a year ago; I didn't enlighten them."

"You didn't tell them!" Eve ejaculated.

Barry looked at her thoughtfully; he gave no other sign of having heard her.

"We were a couple of months at their base, and then they moved up to South Georgia," he finished, "and after a while a whaler brought me home."

"The newspapers never got it—you didn't want them to?" Keith asked. Again Barry did not answer. He seemed not to have heard Keith.

"And Dr. Sassoon was lost," Norah said in a low, troubled voice. Her eyes and Barry's met; seemed to hang together, and she saw again his gentler expression.

"He made a magnificent fight for it," Barry said.

There was a slight pause, which Eve broke:

"But I can't believe it, your coming back!"

"All I wanted was to get here," Barry observed after a while. He looked up at the house. "It's a lovely old place, Foxaway, isn't it?" he said to Norah. But his tone was dull, lifeless.

Chapter XXIII

SHE hardly knew what she answered, or if she answered him at all. Presently she went to the kitchen to consult with the awed and excited Pauline about lunch—the cold corned beef, the asparagus, the cherry pie. When she came out to the side lawn under the elms again, David met her. His face looked drawn.

"Norah, I'm moving along!" he began. Norah, close beside him, looking up at him intently, could make no answer. Her eyes were troubled and anxious.

"How'd you ever happen to marry him, Norah? He isn't a bit like what I thought he was: he isn't your kind. And he's old," said the twenty-five-year-old David wretchedly, "he must be near forty or fifty!"

"He's ten years older than I am. He's thirty-five."

"Well——" David conceded indifferently. Suddenly he burst out, "Norah, you can't go through with it?"

Her color rose; Norah narrowed her eyes and looked away.

"What can I do?" she asked in a whisper.

"Norah, you never loved him?"

"I hardly knew him—how could I?"

"But what *possessed* you!" David exclaimed despairingly. And again Norah could only answer, "I don't know."

"Shall you just—stay on here, with him?" the boy presently demanded.

"I suppose so."

"Norah, how can you! It's terrible!" David muttered.

"I'm so sorry. I'm terribly sorry!" Norah could only repeat stupidly. Her head felt confused. "I don't know what he—wants," she confessed childishly. "I—you can see, he's all broken up, he's tired—inside, I mean, his heart and his mind!"

"Wasn't he always like this?" David demanded suspiciously.

"Well—he was always—" she could find no better term than her old one for him, "he was always pouncing," she said.

"He couldn't possibly expect you to just—stay along here," David said, in strong distaste. "It's—there's no sense to it. He must know—he must see——"

His voice broke; he stooped toward her, half-encircled her with his arm.

"Norah, I'm so terribly fond of you!" he said.

"Oh, I know——" she murmured vaguely, remotely. David and his young love-making already seemed like things belonging to another life. "You see," Norah added, with a little hesitation, "this changes everything. He's unhappy—he's always been unhappy, even when he was quite little. His mother died, and he missed her so! And I can't—I can't just walk out on him!"

"I don't think he especially wants you to stay here!" David said. The girl's sensitive face flushed.

"That's his manner, that teasing, provoking sort of way he has—he doesn't mean anything by it," she explained. "He stood by me when I was down and out," Norah went on, after a pause, "and I can't throw him down now that he is. He *is* down and out, I can see it. And coming here, and finding us all so happy—rejoicing over Foxaway, not missing him a bit, not wanting him—I don't wonder he—got contrary."

"Come down to my mother now, anyway," David urged. "Until things get straightened out. She'd love to have you. Just—get out of it all!"

"Oh, David, don't you see I can't? Don't you see everything is in enough of a mess *now,* without my doing anything *more?*" the girl demanded tragically. "I don't feel the way I did sixteen months ago; maybe he doesn't either. His heart's broken over Sassoon——"

"Who the hell is Sassoon—— Oh, you mean the old guy he went off with? He didn't seem to me heartbroken, the way he was sort of laughing and grinning all the time," David muttered suspiciously.

They stood still for a moment, unhappy and silent. They had strayed through the side garden gate and were standing near David's roadster. David would not stay for lunch, he was going away, and he told her gruffly, awkwardly, that it was forever.

"I've been so damn happy!" he muttered, not looking at her.

"I know."

"Driving up here to see you, telling Mother and Dad yesterday. They were so swell about it!"

"I know."

He looked at her pathetically; their troubled eyes met.

"Gee, what a break!" he said.

"We couldn't see this coming."

"Nobody could have seen this coming!"

"I thought of it—last year. But lately I never thought of it at all," Norah said.

"Will you go on here now, Norah?"

"I don't know."

He turned back from his car.

"If ever you need me—if ever—you know, something might happen," David said, with youthful ineloquence. "If it does, will you let me know, Norah?" He looked down at his steering wheel, moved the accelerator to and fro with his thumb; his face was moody. "I'll never like any-

WIFE FOR SALE

one else: that's over for me. But if ever I could do something for you——"

"You're awfully kind," Norah said thickly. She felt tears sting her eyes. "I was so happy this morning," she added, "I thought everything was going to be so wonderful! And now——"

Again they were silent for a space. Then David said:

"Well, I'll go along. Good-bye, Norah."

He put his big arms about her tightly, crushed her, small and fragrant and tumbled, to his heart. Norah laid a hand on his shoulder, accepted his hard quick kisses on her mouth; she made no response.

And presently David freed her, and got into his car, and went away. Tears were in his eyes, but in Norah's eyes, thoughtfully watching his car disappear down the road, there were no tears.

She walked back to the group on the lawn. Keith had disappeared. Eve was sitting silent, her face a mask of puzzled, proud annoyance. Mrs. Oliver was nervously conducting a conversation with the explorer.

"Howard go?" Barry asked Norah, with his alert look and his inevitable little tag of laughter.

"He had to go."

"Old friend, eh?"

In answer Norah stretched a brown slim hand

toward him, displaying the engagement ring on her wedding finger.

"Well, I timed my arrival nicely, didn't I?" Barry said. Eve caught a quick eager breath, looked at him expectantly, her lips parted. Mrs. Oliver faltered, "You see, nobody *dreamed*——" and fell silent. Norah spoke.

"I forgot to give that back to David!" she said in a mild tone, as if speaking to herself. And quite naturally she continued to Barry, "It must seem—unreal, being back here, after all you've been through!"

Whenever she addressed him it was to be seen his face changed; it was as if, against his will, his shell of shrewd and laughing irony was for a second pierced.

"It was an experience," he admitted briefly.

"You must be tired," Norah suggested.

For answer he rumpled his hair impatiently, laughed.

"It isn't that. No, I'm not tired. I'm just in from a long ocean trip; I came from Australia. There was nothing particularly *tiring* about it."

"These—whalers brought you from South Georgia to Australia?"

"We were several months at their base, farther south. Then we came up, and I worked there for a month or two."

"And no one identified you?"

"There was no reason they should. I'd lost my

clothes, my papers, even my glasses. Something has happened to my eyes; they're stronger than they were. I worked along in the factory with the boys; they called me Otto. They didn't care any more about me than I did about them. Two months ago a boat came up, and I shipped on her. And from Australia I came second class."

"How long were you on the berg, all of you?"

Instead of answering, Barry laughed his gnomelike laugh.

"You don't have to make talk with me, Norah!"

Norah reddened; answered sharply:

"No, and you don't have to be rude!"

"Norah!" her mother ejaculated, scandalized, but Barry's laugh this time had a more genuine note.

"I'm all shaken up," he said apologetically. "I'm sorry!"

"You're home now," Norah reminded him, "you can rest. You can get your bearings."

"No, I'm not home," he answered sadly, darkly. Eve's look of suspicion and scorn changed to one of puzzlement, and she glanced at her mother, who was obviously distressed. But Norah was serene.

"Foxaway is home," she said calmly.

"I can't stay here!" Barry exclaimed restlessly, glancing about.

Keith came down and joined them.

"What's the plot?" he asked, sitting down. His tone was cheerful, casual, yet it was resolute, too. Eve and her mother exchanged fearful glances; Barry looked up moodily at Keith.

"How do you mean what's the plot?" he asked.

"Well, do we clear out?" Keith said. "What do you want us to do? I'm sailing for Guatemala anyway, in about ten days. My mother may come with me——"

There was a pause; a somewhat awkward silence. Then Barry said: "What's the plan, Norah?"

"Why, lunch, of course!" Norah answered composedly. "We're all starving."

"Lunch, of course!" Barry told the others, with a triumphant chuckle.

"We'll bring it out here, we often do," Norah pursued. "Keith, bring the table over. Barbara, you come in with me, and we'll get things. I think I've been smelling biscuits!"

Normality seemed to return to them all. Mrs. Oliver remarked somewhat quaveringly that they often had their meals out here, nowadays, and always had summer breakfasts and suppers under the big tree. Barry sat down again and watched the expert preparations for the meal with his twinkling, narrowed glance. Even Eve unbent, reaching for the pitcher Norah brought down.

"Where are you going with it?" Barry demanded.

"Spring house," Eve answered languidly. "That's my job." And she sent him a lazy smile. Keith meanwhile had drawn a chair close to Barry's, was deep in polar history.

Presently they were all discussing the cold corned beef, the hot biscuits, the home-made jam. Barry was evidently ravenous, and he mellowed under the influence of the good, simple food.

"This wasn't the jam that sugared, was it, Norah?"

"Oh, I wrote you about that, didn't I?"

"To Hobart. And they sent my stuff up, did they?" Barry mused.

"It came yesterday, Judge Bailey said." Norah's eyes brightened. "Oh, *he'll* be glad you're safely back!" she exclaimed.

Barry made no comment on this, merely shrugged. But she saw his thin face flush a little in spite of himself.

"And Hazel didn't care for the will?"

"She wanted Foxaway. She wanted to live here."

"Fiddlesticks!" Barry ejaculated forcefully. "She never had the slightest feeling for the place until I was telling her last October that I intended to live here."

"Maybe it was Lucille Swann who influenced

her," Norah suggested mildly, and at the name they all broke into laughter; rather nervous and shaken laughter, to be sure, but genuine enough for all that. "She said she was engaged to you, you know."

"Lucille Swann!" Barry ejaculated. "Engaged to me, eh?"

"She's been getting a lot of—oh, publicity," Eve supplied. "The newspapers and everything!"

"And how did you like that?" Barry asked Norah.

Norah was scarlet, but she managed a laugh.

"I thought she was probably—that sort of girl."

"I see." As usual, he watched Norah closely for some seconds after she spoke, and when he himself spoke again his voice was lower. "It's a risky thing, this return from the dead!" he said.

Chapter XXIV

AFTER luncheon he sat in his basket chair with his eyes closed. They thought him asleep and were careful to make no noise that would disturb the thin, insignificant figure with the sunken eyes and nervous long-fingered hands. Mrs. Oliver went quietly upstairs for her usual afternoon rest; the girls gathered in the kitchen for dish-washing.

"Norah, what's going to happen now?" Eve asked.

"What should happen now?"

"Will he just—stay on here with us?"

"I suppose so. It's his house."

"It's your house—oh, no; it's his house," Eve conceded reluctantly. "Then we'll all have to get out," she said.

"I don't know. It's all so unexpected."

"Norah, why did you tell him you were engaged to David?" Eve said suddenly.

"I had to tell him, silly."

"You've broken David's heart."

"He'll get over it."

"Norah, you'll have to get out of this—this marriage! It's too awful. David's told his father and mother—and everything——"

Pauline and Eve watched Norah curiously; Norah went on washing dishes without comment.

"You can't go on with it!"

"I was of age and in my right mind," Norah said.

"But, my dear. Why, he's dreadful! Everything he says he grins like a hobgoblin, and he's evidently a nervous *wreck*. And when I think how happy we were, just this morning——" Eve lamented.

"He was always like that."

"But what do you intend to do—*stay* here?" Eve all but shrieked.

"I don't know. He'll have some plan. There's no use going into hysterics about it, Eve. He's come back, and this is his home and I'm his—I'm married to him, and that's all there is about it."

"Oh, believe me, there's lots more to it!" Eve said bitterly. "If you throw a fellow—a *prince* like David Howard down——"

"Don't talk like a child, Eve!" Norah said impatiently. "This isn't a *flirtation!*" She untied her apron, went out to the chairs under the trees again. Keith was sitting there talking to Barry. Norah took a chair, and smiled at them, and wiped her hot forehead.

"Like summer!" she said.

"Norah, take me upstairs!" Barry said suddenly, jumping up. "I've got to wash my face and hands, clean up a little. I've got a bag here, somewhere. We've got to straighten out this whole thing, and I can't do anything until I change."

Keith came toward the house with them, lifted Barry's shabby old leather valise from the doorway, and would have carried it upstairs. But the other man deterred him.

"Thanks awfully, Keith, I'll take that. Norah and I have lots to say to each other. You go ahead, Norah, I don't know the way. Which is our room?"

If the possessive pronoun shocked her she gave no sign. From the wide upper hall she went through the open door into a pleasant airy farmhouse chamber; pear-tree blossoms made a white tapestry at the window.

"This is my room," Norah said, without expression. "Have you a brush and comb? Wait; you'd like some hot water!"

She went into the hall, called down.

"Pauline, will you bring up some hot water?"

"This was my mother's room when I was a kid," Barry said. How far was he really at ease, really smiling, as he briskly went about his washing and dressing, Norah confusedly wondered. How much of the earthquake within her mind and soul was she betraying?

She sat in a flounced old winged chair at one

of the big eastern windows. "I am as smart as you are—you can't bluff me!" she thought in her trembling heart. Aloud she said:

"Do you mind my sitting here watching you?"

"I like it," Barry answered. "We're married, you know."

She could be as nonchalant as he.

"That's what I was thinking."

Norah's eyes wandered. She looked out of the window.

"I love this view."

"How'd you know this was my mother's room?"

Her vague glance returned.

"Oh—Huldy, I guess. Huldy Barnard."

"Huldy take good care of you when you first came up?"

"It was a little slow, getting everything started. She wasn't well, you know."

"But she had the rooms all warm and ready, everything comfortable?"

"It was all right."

"Eve wrote me differently!" Barry observed, with his elfin chuckle. Norah's bright color rose, and she laughed too at her own expense.

"My sister Eve did?"

"Yes, to Hobart, in the very beginning. She was indignant, as I remember it. She wanted me to let you off the whole bargain."

"She didn't know we had been married, then."

"No, and that makes a difference, doesn't it?"

Barry was clean-shaven now; his hair sleekly combed. He looked younger, if still tired and thin.

"Certainly," Norah said gallantly.

They walked to the door.

"Going to like being married to me, Norah?" Barry said, in the hall.

"I hope so," Norah answered sedately.

"It's one thing to make a bargain and another to fulfil it, isn't it?" the man asked.

"Rather!" Norah agreed cheerfully, politely.

She said immediately that she wanted to show him some changes she had made here and there in the house and garden. But not now, not until later.

"It is so heavenly at about five," she told him. "That's the time to see everything."

"Norah, what's making you nervous?"

"Nothing," she said, with a surprised glance that was perfection in its pleasant gravity.

She heard him chuckle as he followed her down to the lawn; her mother and brother and sister were gathered there in the warm afternoon peace. Norah and Barry found chairs; Barry, who looked pale and tired, stretched himself out wearily; she leaned from her own chair to put a pillow under his head, and he opened the eyes he had closed in his rather cadaverous face and nodded his thanks.

"We've been talking, Mr. Dunsmuir," Keith began. "And my mother and Eve and I rather think we ought to get out."

A pause; Barry opened his eyes, spoke in a faintly irritated tone.

"Why get out? You people are very comfortable here. Why not let me get out?"

"That's nonsense!" Keith said with an uncomfortable laugh.

"All places are alike to me," Barry observed. Norah indulged in a brief, barely audible laugh. "What's funny?" he asked, moving his eyes toward her.

"You are," Norah answered noncommittally.

"You all like Foxaway," Barry resumed in an annoyed, tired voice, "and Norah here thought it was hers no longer ago than this morning. I've no use for it. I'm planning another trip, anyway. I may be in England for a year, on research work."

Mrs. Oliver, with a resoluteness most unusual in her, suddenly took charge of the conversation.

"No, I think we'll go down to the city, or to my daughter in Scarsdale, Mr. Dunsmuir," she decided pleasantly, soothingly; "and give you a little time to get your bearings. You've had a terrible experience, and a long trip, and I think that will be the best arrangement, for a while anyway. Keith—my son," she nodded at him with the expression of complete pride with which she always pronounced the two words, "will be leaving for Guatemala very soon anyway, and I want to get him some things in the city."

Barry had opened his eyes; they were fixed politely on her.

"As you like," he responded politely, when she paused.

"We'll be back——" Norah began uncomfortably. Barry's look moved to her.

"Oh, are you going, Norah?" he asked, in a level, interested tone. The girl's color came up in a rush under her brown firm skin, and her involuntary laugh had a startled note. She glanced at her mother.

"Well, I—I don't know!" she stammered. Mrs. Oliver was equal to the moment.

"I think Norah had better come with us, if you are going to have a real rest——" she began confidentially, and stopped. Her own color rose, as Norah's had. "Of course," she recommenced, in a fluttered voice, "Norah's—I'd forgotten that, or rather I can't somehow realize it——"

"You mean Norah's being my wife?" Barry asked.

"She only told me a few weeks ago," Keith put in. "And my mother only this morning."

"And Norah would prefer to go down with you and then perhaps come back?" Barry pursued idly.

"Well, all this is exciting—it's unexpected," Mrs. Oliver pleaded staunchly. A little nervous spot of color burned in each cheek. "If she had had a little time to prepare for it," she went on, "it would be different. But Norah's always been like a—like a child about some things, Mr. Dunsmuir. She has had time now to consider that—that marriage of hers——"

"I was twenty-four, darling!" Norah herself said in an absent-minded undertone.

"I know, dear. But you were a *child!*" the mother reiterated eagerly.

"I wasn't anything of the kind," Norah protested, her affectionate laugh and tone taking the edge from the words. "I knew what I was doing."

"Unfortunately," Mrs. Oliver said with dignity, "that was just what you didn't know. You were married without time to reflect and without consulting me. If you *had* consulted me, the marriage never would have taken place!"

"Mr. Dunsmuir would hardly hold Norah to anything she didn't want to do!" Eve now said lightly, significantly.

"Mr. Dunsmuir wouldn't think of disappointing your expectations of him," Barry assured her instantly, with his narrowed smile. "Norah is as free as you are. She will, of course, go down with you all this afternoon."

"It seems to me the sensible thing," Mrs. Oliver agreed quickly. "When you are rested, when things are all straightened out, then we can see what's wisest to be done."

"What do you think, Norah?" Barry asked, with a hint of his old grin. From her silence, her flushed face and lowered eyes, he could read the tumult in her soul; in the look she suddenly gave him he saw pride and fear and puzzlement mingled.

"Norah knows that her mother never would have sanctioned a secret marriage with a man she hardly knew," her mother answered for her.

"You think I took an advantage of Norah?" Barry asked.

"I think such a marriage is always a mistake, Mr. Dunsmuir."

"You mean you would like it canceled, the marriage?" Barry asked interestedly. His tone betrayed neither reluctance nor regret; it was almost as if he were enjoying himself.

"Unfortunately," Mrs. Oliver answered with dignity, "that is not possible. But some arrangement, between you and Norah, or you and her brother——"

"Norah entered into one understanding with me sixteen months ago," Barry said temperately. "Now she doesn't want to keep that bargain, she wants to make another. Well, that's all right with me. What is the new bargain?"

He paused, with an eloquent shrug. Norah spoke in the pause. Her tone was angry and proud.

"What makes you think I don't want to keep it?"

After an electric moment Mrs. Oliver said sharply:

"Norah!"

"Mother, it was a bargain."

"Yes, but—circumstances—Mr. Dunsmuir's absence——"

"Exactly!" Barry agreed, with twinkling eyes. "Can't you see that everything's changed?"

"No," Norah said simply, with a level glance at him, "I can't. You go down with Keith tomorrow, Mother, and take Eve. And if you go back to Guatemala, I'll come down and see you off. I'll stay here."

"Bravo!" Barry said, in the ironic voice she hated.

"I think Mr. Dunsmuir's suggestion is much the better, dear. We'll leave him here for a good rest, and then later on—possibly——"

"That wasn't my bargain," Norah said, in a cool, disinterested voice. "Barry's quite right—it's easy to promise a thing and—sometimes hard to perform it. But—" she looked at him, "if he wants me," she said, "I'll stay here."

"I don't say—just a moment, I didn't say I wanted you," Barry said, trying to laugh. Norah, looking gravely at him, was surprised to see that his forehead was wet with perspiration and that he was trembling. "That isn't the point, is it? The point is that we agreed——"

"We agree now, for the matter of that," she interrupted him. "Don't discuss it any more. The others will go. I stay."

She got up and stooped from behind her mother's chair to kiss Mrs. Oliver's forehead.

"I'm going up the spring trail, Mother, to—to think about things. Too much has happened—too fast. I'll not be long. Don't discuss this any more. It's settled."

A slender figure in dark blue ruffles, with a brimmed hat of brown straw deep over her gray eyes, she looked from one face to the other: Keith's handsome troubled face, Eve's stormy forehead and bitten lip. When she came to Barry she smiled.

"It was so nominated in the bond!" she said, and was gone. For a long time none of the four persons she left behind her moved or spoke.

Chapter XXV

She had not reached the little turn into the lane by the stile before she knew that Barry was following her. Norah looked at him over her shoulder, waited, and they walked along together up the path and to the spring pool.

The hot afternoon had reached a moment of arrestment; all the glow and beauty and perfume of the world stood still in a shaft of westering light. No leaf stirred; no bird called; the streamers of the descending sun had fixed every flower, every spray of fruit blossom and spear of grass in a pellucid clear glow; they were transfixed in a bath of air as clear as pond water or as crystal.

Only the waters of the brook came swiftly tumbling down over stones to the pool by the spring, and flung eternally into the warm air a fine cooling mist that rose in vapor from the foaming little waterfall. Norah and Barry sat down on the great birch log that was half embedded in the pool, and Norah took off her straw hat and fanned her glowing face.

"May first!" she said, opening a casual conversation.

"It gets terribly hot here at Foxaway, doesn't it?"

"Never any hotter than this. At least, you never feel it as you do these first hot days. Oh, in August," Norah conceded, "when we take our lunch and go up to the Lake early, then it's hot when we come back, the house gets hot. But we never minded it! We used to swim in the evenings last summer, sometimes. Or we'd have supper here by the spring pool."

"What fun you've had out of the old place!"

"I believe some women are countrywomen, and some naturally thrive in the cities," Norah observed, smiling. "The night we got here—and since Eve wrote you about it, I may as well admit it was rather awful!—but even that night, I had a feeling—a *feeling* that I'd never had before. It was getting home."

"Mother like it?" Barry asked, watching the light in her eyes, studying the smooth firm lines of the brown face, and the movements of her red mouth.

"Mother and Eve were—ghastly."

"Hated it?"

"Oh, Barry, Huldah was deathly sick, it was bitter cold outside, with snow, there was no fire in the kitchen, no food, everything smelled of rats and rotting wood and cold ashes, could you blame Mother and Eve?"

He laughed.

"But you liked it?"

"Liked it!" she echoed, in a tone of infinite content.

For under all the flurry and confusion of her thoughts Norah was content. Quite suddenly and simply she had seen her path clear, had known not only what she must do, but that it was what she wanted to do. This was her world; this thin, wistful, contrary man was her man. She asked nothing more.

"I've been—kind of—saving up nerves and meanness and everything else just until I got back here, I guess," Barry presently said, in a silence. His tone was different, apologetic. He ended with a mirthless brief laugh.

Norah had apparently not heard him.

"If we'd thought of it, we could have had supper up here tonight," she said dreamily.

The man spoke simply, seriously.

"I used to wish they'd do that, when I was little."

"Have supper up here by the pool?"

"Yes, but they never did."

"Who were the grown-ups here then, Barry?"

"My uncle, Dr. Dunsmuir—and, until I was ten, my mother."

Norah was silent. Barry wiped his wet forehead.

"It's beginning to break," the girl said, of the languorous, lingering day. "It'll be marvelous in a few minutes, and tonight there's a full moon."

Barry spoke abruptly.

"Listen!" he said. "Of course I have no idea of keeping you to that marriage—you know that! You know I was just—amusing myself."

Norah looked at him thoughtfully, looked away.

"Fred Sassoon!" he burst out wretchedly. "He was the only person I ever cared about, except my mother. He was the biggest of them all: they'll never know it! He used to consult me, Norah—Fred Sassoon consulting a wretched, blinking, ignorant fool like me! He'd come into the Commons—that was where four of us bunked on the *Ladysmith,* and he'd get a pencil and charts——

"He was so happy! He'd always wanted to do just that; cruise around down there, get down as far as Ross Bay. And then he lost Cotton, you know, at Hobart—that almost killed him—and he put me in. The night before—I'll never forget it—I walked the streets. They were leaving in three days, and I'd not been asked to go along! And then Cotton died, and the Chief said, 'Thank God you're here, Barry!'

"Then old Arnesen died, our best engineer. He'd been with Scott and Shackleton on some of their trips. That was another blow to the Chief. And after that——"

He was silent. After a while Norah said:

"That was why you didn't want anyone to identify you. The newspapers—the excitement—and Dr. Sassoon not in it."

Barry said nothing. There was a trough below the spring pool, and now four cows slumped awkwardly down through a daisy meadow and stopped at the water. The sun sent their long shadows ten feet ahead of them.

"Whose cows?"

"Ours. But I've been pasturing the Abbots' too, all winter. I had the Tafts' Johnny come up every night and feed them and milk. And I've boarded dogs," Norah said. "And Pauline and I put up the famous jam that sugared, and we've sold flowers and cream—cream and broilers to the hotel, and we had a dollar-and-a-half Sunday dinner for a while." She laughed. "That was *frightful!*" she said.

He was looking at her with the old look she remembered, a look of eager interest in her talk.

"You've lived every minute of it," he said. "But then, you see, you've had your mother and brother and sister——"

"Not always. Keith only came up for Thanksgiving; then he was gone until March. Eve's away a lot. But I've had Barbara and Binge——"

Norah dropped her slim brown hand to the

dog's head, and Binge made a delicately moaning sound of pure adoration and ecstasy.

"I've been ill," Barry presently burst out. "I've not slept. All the way home I've been in a sweat to get to Foxaway. And then this morning to get here—and feel everything wrong, everything vaguer than ever——

"I don't know! It's in me, I guess, or rather there's something lacking from me. I've been sick for just these three—just this sort of spring day, and yet——

"Yet I come back to annoy you, Norah, and drive the man you love away from you and make you unhappy!"

"You couldn't very well not come home, Barry," she said mildly.

"I broke into your room," he said, "I tried to make you back down; I couldn't."

"I knew what you were trying to do."

"I didn't do it. Norah," Barry said, with a sudden change of manner, "I must ask you something. I'm not teasing you now—I want to help you. How much do you like David Howard?"

"Not very much."

"No, tell me the truth."

"That is the truth."

"But weren't you engaged to him?"

"Well, yes—but that was before you came back."

"No, seriously, my dear," Barry said. "You don't have to say that. You are married to me technically, of course. But there are circumstances that would make an annulment a very simple thing. I know that."

"I'm not saying it for any reason except that it's true. I *did* have a—well, a terrible case on him," Norah admitted. "But that was years ago. This year he's been the one to—to take it seriously. I would have married him, perhaps—but I was always putting it off; I didn't want to leave Foxaway. And when Judge Bailey came this morning—we told you about that—and said that you had—had left me everything—that they had found the will you wrote in Hobart——"

She stopped. Her lashes were wet, but she was smiling.

"Then the first thing I thought of," she resumed after a moment, "was that I wouldn't have to marry anyone."

"I've been acting like a fool all day," Barry said. "But I was tired. I'd reached the end of my road and found—found that I didn't belong there. But I'll not worry you any more, Norah. I'm going to make this place over to you, as you thought I had by my death, and then I'll get out."

There was a silence.

"Let's go back to our meeting each other sixteen—seventeen months ago," Norah said. "I was down and out. I advertised——"

"We know all that!" he interposed as she paused.

"I know we do. But I advertised for some man that would be good to my mother, help me take care of her, and I said that I would marry that man if we liked each other. I said that marriage was a serious thing to me, that I would do my best to make his home a real home and make him happy."

"It hasn't turned out that way," Barry said.

"I think it has! Here is the home," Norah said, "and I've worked over every inch of it—the attics and the parlor and the garden. And here you are, home, and here am I."

"And we are not the same persons we were eighteen months ago."

"No, but that doesn't matter. We hardly knew each other then. There's no reason we should have less courage now!"

"Do we know each other better now?"

"I know *you* better!" Norah answered confidently. "I used to think," she went on, "that of all the men who didn't need a wife you were the—the shining example! I thought that you were a born bachelor, and I thought——"

He was sitting on a rock just behind and above the sunken log she had chosen for her own seat; they had both been looking down the wooded slope to the roofs and fences of the farm, all mellowed in shadowless twilight now, and seen through the delicate screen of the new leaves. Norah turned, and her bright face was close to his own as he leaned toward her.

"I thought, in those very first days," she resumed, "that of all the men who could possibly have answered my letter—that first newspaper letter, saying that I'd marry anyone, and all that —I thought that of all the *possible* men you were really the one I had least expected, the one I was least able to deal with!"

"You expected a movie hero," he said, with a touch of hurt, a hint of shrinking, in his voice.

"Well, I suppose I did," the girl answered, smiling, after a moment's thought. "It's a regular movie story! But it wasn't that, so much," she went on, "as that you were so smart, Barry—you were older than I, and so quick, and so—so pouncing. I always think of you as pouncing on me!"

"You didn't want a fool, I suppose?"

"No. That's just the point. But I thought I did! And David," Norah admitted, frowning a little, smiling a little at the same time, "is— to all intents and purposes, a fool."

She had laid her hand on his knee; now his fingers covered it.

"David is?" he asked, clearing his throat.

"Yes," she answered decidedly. "I don't mean

that he isn't nice, and handsome, and rich, and —and really very fond of me," Norah conceded. "But in every mental and spiritual way he simply—isn't there. The things he says about clothes and shows and taxes and cigarettes and cocktails and motorcars and guns and comic strips are just what everyone else says, and he isn't interested in anything else!"

"But I thought—" Barry began a little huskily, "I thought you and I disagreed, too, Norah, about—well, God, for one thing, and —oh, well, about woman's place in the big scheme——"

"As for God," Norah answered calmly, in the pause, "I've come to see that one explanation of men's—men's essential—essential inferiority to women is that they have to find God through women—through a woman. You'll find God. Wait until your work's going well and you come out to find me bargaining for gooseberry plants, next spring. Wait a few years more, until we bring little Ellen and Barry and the twins and the baby up here, and let them wade——"

Barry used both hands to press his handkerchief over his eyes.

"I guess I'm a little weak, still!" he said, in a trembling voice, when he could face her again.

"A woman can do a great deal for a man," Norah observed, "without writing operas or painting masterpieces for him!"

Barry laughed shakily, catching at her hand again.

"But, Norah, Norah, you don't know me! You don't know that you even like me!"

"As I've come to know you better," the girl persisted, "I've come to like you—to understand you, better than I ever did anyone in my life!"

He stared at her, puzzled.

"What are you talking about, Norah? How can you possibly know me better than you did?"

"I know you because I found all your journals, from your sixth to your seventeenth year," Norah said calmly.

"My God!" Barry ejaculated, with a horrified glance.

"I thought you were dead," Norah pursued. "I thought that—as your wife——"

"Lots of them were just a few pages," he said uncomfortably.

"Oh, yes, you'd skipped lots. But I read about the little boy that used to pretend he had lots of sisters and brothers. And I read about the tenth birthday party."

She looked at him fairly.

"It made me cry," she confessed. And now her brown hand went out, and she laid it on his. "I found out in those diaries," she went on, "what's the matter with you—why you act so—so silly sometimes, and are always laughing and —getting off—smart cracks!"

WIFE FOR SALE

The touch of her hand had changed him; his keen eyes were soft, his voice humble as he turned to her.

"Why do I act so, Norah?"

"Because you're shy, Barry. Because those beastly cousins and uncles of yours made you self-conscious—made you miserable, when you were only a lonely little boy. You were smarter than they, and you knew it, and you developed this—this armor of—whatever it is——"

"Smart cracks," he supplied.

"Well, self-defense. And, Barry," Norah cleared her throat, but her voice remained husky, "Barry, you like me very much, don't you?" she asked.

He smiled; blinked wet eyelashes.

"Do I?"

"Yes, you do."

"What makes—what makes you think so?"

"The dreadful—the *abominable* way you've been acting all day!" Norah said, and they both laughed shakily.

"I like you so much, my dear, that I couldn't make you unhappy," Barry told her, in the simplest manner she had ever seen him use. There was a pause.

"But do you like me enough to make me happy?"

"Ah, Norah, I could never do that."

"All the time I was putting Foxaway in

order," she presently told him, "fixing your books, reading them, finding the places you had said in the diaries you liked—finding even your little water-color sketch for your mother's birthday—the sketch of the parlor, do you remember? I made the whole room over, to have it as you knew it—all that time I was finding you, thinking of the boy who wanted to write books.

"So you see I know you, Barry, and you can never fool me again! I know what it means to you to sit here and see the blossoms on the fruit trees, and the barns, and hear the screen door on the kitchen bang, and smell the grass, and the smoke going up from the chimney."

"Some day I'll come back," he said, trembling.

"You'll not go away. The others will—but you and I will stay here—just ourselves. And you'll rest, Barry, and wander about here, and we'll bring our suppers up into the woods, or take them over to the Lake shore. And when you can't sleep at night," Norah said, tears in her smiling eyes, "your wife will be there to talk to—to keep you from being lonely."

"And frightened," he whispered, smiling; but his face was wet; "frightened for Fred Sassoon —thinking——"

"And some day," Norah said, "you'll do him —do Fred Sassoon in a biography. Who else could, Barry? You knew him, you were with him until almost the end, you know what he thought and said. That'll be your tribute to him; the thing only you can do. Your name—you knew that?—was the last word he wrote."

"I know," he said.

"Could you do that, Barry?"

"I don't know."

The sun was gone now; the fragrant May world was washed with clear shadowless light. Bees, chickens, birds, were all silent; except when a whippoorwill called liquidly in the near woods.

"It wouldn't be fair to you, Norah."

"Nothing else would be fair to me!"

"It would be heaven to be here with you."

"It *is* heaven!

"When I first came," she presently began again, as he was silent, "I felt—every fiber of me—that I belonged here. I remember coming out of that barn door down there on one of the first days just at dusk, when it was going to snow, and feeling like shouting—feeling like flying, because it was Foxaway and I was here.

"Lately, just these last few months, you've been here too. I've thought of you—dead, and never having had your happy times here, your picnics at the pool, or taking your mattress up to the nine-acre meadow."

"You found that too?"

"I tell you I know you through and through.

And now, today, you come back," Norah went on, "still a shy little boy wanting to be loved—not knowing quite how to manage it—contrary and stupid——"

He was on his knees beside her on the grass, his arms locked about her.

"Norah, I'll make you love me! I'll live to make you happy! You shall have everything you want—your mother here, Barbara—I'll love them—I love to have the old rooms full! We'll have fires, and Christmas feasts, and we'll read books together. But be kind to me now; don't send me away. I could have borne it a few hours ago, but I couldn't go now! No one has ever talked to me this way; no one has ever been so divinely, so heavenly kind to me as you have been, just this hour! I've seen—I've seen the gate of heaven open!"

She was stroking his hair: thick stubborn hair full of tough curls.

"I'll never let you go," she assured him, in her tender young motherly voice. "I've been trying to tell you—it isn't what I thought it was going to be—but I've been trying to tell you——"

"What?" he whispered, for Norah had stopped short as if she could never go on.

"That I love you, I suppose. It's—queer," Norah confessed simply. "It's more like a possession, or a fever, than being happy—than having a case. But it's—that."

"I worship you," he said in a shaking voice. "I worship you. My whole life changes tonight. Nothing else matters—nothing else so important has ever come to me. I never thought it would come! I never dreamed anyone so lovely—so infinitely—*dear,* could ever be! Norah, I'll live for you—there'll be nothing else——

"It means that everything—everything that's gone before is worth while—everything's been right—leading up to this. . . ."

There was a silence. Their eyes clung together. Norah marked the two half circles of his heavy brows with delicate fingertips.

"Feathers!" she said, smiling a mother's smile.

"Norah, must we ever go back to them, the others?"

"They'll be gone in a day or two."

"I can't—I can't end this hour."

"I've *got* to. Dessert is sponge cake and jam, and I make the sponge cake! But afterward—there's a moon. Shall you and I walk up to the meadow above here and see it rise? Or are you too tired?"

"I am winged!" he said.

"Then we'll slip away," she said. "But we must go down now."

She stood beside him a minute, and the smile Barry gave her she thought might be the same smile a lonely little affectionate diarist had given his invalid mother years ago.

"I'm happy, Barry!" the girl said.

"I can't believe I'm awake. I'm on an iceberg somewhere, going off into coma."

"You're wide awake."

"And it's you and I for the rest of the chapter?" he said.

"Me and my hubsand!" she said.

They went down the slope and past the stile, and so to Foxaway farmhouse together.